About the Author

Nathan Eden graduated from university at the end of the last century, and has lived and worked in various countries, both as a child and as a sometimes-functioning adult.

Married with three sons, Tom, Jonny and Zach, Nathan spends much of his time trying (and failing) to understand teenagers and keep up with a rampaging toddler.

Splintered

Acknowledgements

Life is busy, there is no doubt about that. For years, actually, decades, I'd promised myself I'd follow up on my love of reading other people's books, and, one day, write one myself. 'One day' turns in to 'next month', turns in to 'next year', and before you know it, you're breaking a promise to yourself. So, I tried to make life a little less busy for a year or so, and just sat down and started. If there is one bit of advice I could give (and I'm really not qualified to give out much advice... definitely not the good sort anyway), I would say that if there is that one thing that has always been nagging in the back of your mind to do, start now. Take that step to get on the roller-coaster, because once it gets going, you can't get off!

This book wouldn't have happened if not for the support of a few special people. Thanks to Calum Barker, for putting the idea in my head to write things down in the first place (sorry I killed you off). To Rehan Khan (a great author in his own right, and please check out his novels) for the planning advice. To Jennifer Campbell (another great writer) for the motivation to step onto the roller-coaster and for bouncing ideas with. To Jade Sterling for the fancy coffees, ideas, editing, proof reading et cetera, and for generally just being there to keep this project going. To those who inspired a few of the characters in this book. You were in my head every step of the way.

And finally, to my wife, Lindsay, for believing in me.

1
"Faster, Daddy!"

Feeling the summer's first sunshine breaking through the wispy clouds to warm my face, I'm awash with a sense of positivity I've not felt in a long time. Forget everything that's happened to me over the last few years. I can make a fresh start from here. I close my eyes and take a long, deep, contented breath in. In 1, 2, 3, 4, focus on my breathing, and out 1, 2, 3, 4. Just like we practiced.

The thin skin of my eyelids transforms the bright, white sunlight into a more relaxing deep red. Think of something and focus on it. I hear a muffled screeching sound. Not that. Don't think about that. Focus on something else, quickly. A quiet beach. A rustling palm tree. The azure ocean lapping at the white sand beneath my feet. I feel the warm breeze gently finger through my hair, and I can smell the saltiness of the sea around me. That's better, Ollie, that's better.

Another breath. In 1, 2, 3, 4. Focus on the breeze again. Feel the powdery sand scrunch between my toes as I curl them in. Nice. And out 1, 2, 3, 4 and here it comes. Feel that wave of delicious serenity coursing across my chest, melting away the tension in my throat. Feel it.

Somewhere in the depths of my mind, I'm conscious of activity around me. Muffled noises, as if I'm underwater, threatening to invade my ears. Ignore it. Ignore it all. Cling on to this feeling. Everything is going to be OK. Focus.

In 1, 2, 3, 4. More noise, clearer this time. Out 1, 2… Fuck it! I open my eyes and let the outside world flood back in and drown me.

"Why have you stopped?" whines a shrill voice. "Push me, Daddy. I want to go really high this time!"

William is innocent. Carefree. Happy. As every five-year-old child should be. I envy his freedom, the weightlessness on his shoulders. I push him. I love him. His delight is evident from the high-pitched squeals and stupefied smile on his face. When did the simple things become not enough? Why can't I swing my worries away? What even is my swing these days? I feel myself drift away again, subconsciously continuing to push him away each time he returns to me, and a memory fades in.

A grainy, blurred image of a child. It looks like William, but it's not him. Swinging through the air. There's no smile on his face. My face. It's me. I look to the figure behind me – who is pushing? It's Mum, and she isn't smiling either. Just two people going through the motions of life. We do this because it's normal, isn't it? Dad isn't there again. Why isn't he pushing me like I'm pushing William? I try, but no matter what I do, I can't bring him into this vision. I can barely remember what he looked like. He left us when I was young. Too young. About the same age as William is now. Maybe I can bring a smile to Mum's sad face. Focus. Concentrate. No. Things were never simple, even then.

"I'm a bird, Daddy!"

Jolted back to the present. Pushing. Smiling. Mainly because I want to, but also because it's normal, isn't it? To smile. Beyond William, a group of women sit on a red picnic blanket under the shade of a sprawling oak tree. Two of them are talking while greedily spooning what looks like sand into their brightly lip-sticked mouths. The latest middle-class food craze no doubt.

Oh, this is so good, I could eat this for every meal. But you don't, do you? If you did, you probably wouldn't have arses that size, would you? That sort of extra weight takes a lot of consistent effort. A diet rich with remorse, a pinch of self-loathing and a generous helping of processed sugar and saturated fat.

I don't know where this weight is coming from since I cut out gluten. Fuck off.

Of course, I have no idea what they're saying. I can't hear them, and I couldn't read their lips even without the accompanying chomping. But I know enough to be able to fill in the gaps.

The third woman is different. Very different. A different species more different. She sits quietly, alternating between watching them and watching William and me. I know her well enough to know what she's thinking, and it'll be a lot closer to what I've just been thinking. I can sense her feelings are mirroring my own. She is beautiful. Undeniably, breathtakingly beautiful. The rim of her large, straw summer hat droops around her elegant face, her wavy brown hair falling to rest on her tanned shoulders. Her beauty is effortless. A smile. The lines around her mouth hint at time passed, and even though it feels as if from another lifetime, I can still picture that same smile on a younger face.

I didn't even want to go out that night, but Calum was adamant. We walked into the pub on a quiet Tuesday evening, and there was that smile on the other side of the room, shining onto the friend sat next to her. It was the first thing I saw, and I remember feeling a momentous sense that my life was about to change. Love at first sight? Maybe not. That would take a few more hours. Full of confidence and a charm I didn't really know I possessed, Calum walked left towards the bar and I went right, straight over towards the smile and to the rest of my life. Hi.

Our tenth wedding anniversary is coming up soon. Shit, I

mustn't forget that. Not two years in a row. Ten years. There will be a name for ten years. Paper? No, I think we've had paper. That was the first year. In fact, thinking about it, I remember the gift she bought for me that year. Tickets to the football. We've had leather too. I definitely remember that present, or more accurately, the night that involved that present. I wonder what ten years is though. Crystal? Pearl? I'll have to find out. Hopefully it'll be a cheap one. Just don't forget it. I'll need to double check the date too.

The sound of squawking laughter breaks my daydream. I look to my right. A small group of teenagers must have turned up in the last few minutes while I've been in my own head. They're probably fourteen or fifteen years old at most, the boys thinking they are men and the girls thinking they are women. But clearly neither is true. One of the boys is pulling a wheelie on his bike in a juvenile attempt to impress the watching girls. The girls are dressed as if they're going nightclubbing or something, with far too much pre-pubescent flesh on show. Their flat chests and bruised shins hinting at a childhood they haven't finished yet, no matter what they might think. When did teenagers change so much?

It's easy to see the leader of the group. His long, dark fringe hiding one eye, giving himself an aloof sense of intrigue. All the girls are watching him, seemingly unable to break their besotted stares, giggling and whispering to each other, waiting for him to say or do something. So, in fact, are the boys. I can feel a dark hatred towards him take root in my stomach.

Is it as strong as hatred? Maybe it's jealousy. I don't ever remember any of the girls that I knew ever dressing like that. Just be kids, for fuck's sake. Stop trying to grow up so fast. It's fucking shit when you do anyway. Forget the fake crap you're being fed on Facebook and Instagram and whatever other social media sites are big with kids these days. Everyone on there is lying about their lives anyway. Faking their happiness. Faking their success. Faking everything. None of it is true, is it? I feel my shoulders droop and I sigh loudly.

I think I do wish the girls had dressed like that when I was their age. Jealousy, then. Fuckers.

"Daddy stop, stop! The ice cream man!"

Before I can even bring the swing to a stop, William has jumped off and is running towards the approaching ice cream van as it crawls down the road towards us, playing its enticing tunes over its crackly Tannoy. He'll stop any minute, when he realises I'm not right behind him. His little arms pump wildly as he runs.

Bend your elbows kid, you look weird.

Any second now, he'll stop and look for me. Any second. OK, he's not going to. He just keeps running, not even put off when one of his shoes flies off his foot. He'll grow into them, she said. Obviously, you've still got a bit of growing to do, William. I turn towards Becky, that smile now focussed on me. At this distance, I can't actually hear her laugh, but I can see it. She shrugs her shoulders and mouths to me 'go on', nodding her head towards William. Her face contorts into an exaggerated look of comic confusion, her way of saying 'you know we can't control him when he's like this'.

And then a scream. A blood-curdling, skin-tingling scream that sends an icy chill through my veins. I whip my head towards the noise and see William is face down on the floor with a large mountain bike on top of him, the back wheel still spinning as if in silent apology. I sprint to him, eyes fixed on the shoeless little foot poking out from under a greasy pedal.

It's not moving. Why isn't it moving? Why aren't you

moving?

"William!"

I lift the bike off him and throw it to the side, and as I do, I'm relieved to see him finally moving, pushing his little body up to sitting. I kneel beside him to help him up, and hold his shoulders still so that I can assess any damage. He looks to me, his face frantically contorted, eyes wide and brimming with terrified shock, mouth open, screaming silently.

There is blood dripping down his cheek. His beautiful, soft cheek. I'm dizzy. Swimming in a dark water that deadens my senses. Eventually, his scream comes. A long shriek erupts and pierces my ear drums. Tears fill his eyes. Blood. He reaches out to me with both arms, but I ignore his need for comfort, take my hands from his shoulders and turn to look at the bike's rider standing behind me.

The fringe. Concern and embarrassment etched across his face in equal proportions. A fury burns within me, taking control of my body and clouding my thoughts. William's continued screaming galvanises my rage further. I stand, grab the boy's skinny neck with one hand, and with an animalistic fury, I roar, punching him hard in his face with the other. Blood splatters across his shocked face. My left arm aches with the tension of keeping him standing up as his legs give way beneath him. I punch him again. My wrist sears with pain. A watery thud, as my fist smashes his soft face again, pulping it up. Punch. Again, and again. Blood. His eyes roll back into his skull. I keep punching. Again. Again.

"Oliver!" A scream. "Oliver, let go of him!"

The outside world comes racing back to my consciousness. I see my left hand stretched out in front of me, gripping the boy's t-shirt. My right is balled into a white-knuckled fist, tightly coiled behind me. My muscles are twitching to be released.

"Oliver, for God's sake, let go of him!" Becky yells.

I stare at him and a thousand thoughts swirl around my fogged mind.

"I didn't mean it, Mister!" the boy pleads, his teenage voice cracking in terror. "He ran right in front of me. I couldn't dodge him, I'm sorry!"

Fear warps the boy's face, but there is no blood, no rolling eyes, no mashed face. The rage begins to subside within me. My body stays hot, my jaw remains tight, but my mind begins to clear as reality takes a seat in my head. I drop my loaded fist and at the same time let go of him. As quickly as he can, he picks up his bike and runs away from me.

"Fucking psycho!" he screeches back over his shoulder.

I slump as the adrenaline dissipates within me and turn back to William, now wrapped in the safe consoling embrace of his mother. His wails have quietened to a sniffle. A small, irrelevant red scratch on his face. Becky looks at me. Terrified.

2

The drive home is shrouded in a cold, tense silence. I feel like I'm drowning under Becky's ocean of shame and fury. She doesn't say anything to me, and I decide it's best to keep my own mouth shut for the time being. Even William, usually full of childish questions about anything going on outside his backseat window, wisely opts to remain quiet. As soon as I park outside the house, I quickly get out, shut the door behind me and march into the house. I know I am leaving Becky to bring in the picnic stuff from the car, adding further fuel to her already raging fire, but I need to get somewhere I can be alone.

Becky would want to speak to me about what had happened, but I don't need her on my case just yet. I run up the stairs, taking two steps at a time, dart into the bathroom and quickly lock the door behind me. I turn the tap on at the sink, cup my hands under the flowing cold water and scoop it up to splash my face. I do this a few times until I feel the sticky shame has been washed away, straighten up and look in the mirror. The man looking back at me appears cleansed, if only on the surface.

I close my eyes and immediately the image of Becky's shocked face jumps to mind. I've seen her angry before. Plenty of times. Husbands tend to do that to their wives from time to time. I've seen her upset. Again, husbands do that to their wives as well. Over recent years, I have even become used to her looks of apathy and disappointment. But today was different. Frightened. She looked so frightened. Terrified, in fact, and I am filled with shame as a result. I should apologise.

I can hear her downstairs, walking in and out of the house, fetching our stuff from the boot of the car. When the front door eventually slams shut, shaking the front of the house and rattling the bathroom window in its frame, I know she's finished, and I know she's pissed off. I give it a few minutes, hoping she'll cool down a little, before leaving the sanctuary of the bathroom. I walk down the upstairs landing, the walls lined with family photos of better days, down the stairs and into the kitchen, ready for my judgement.

When we were looking at the houses we could afford to rent, in the areas we liked, almost all of them were absolute shitholes. When we moved to London, I think we had both had a romantic image of a fresh start in a beautiful home, with a beautiful garden, hundreds of miles from what we'd left behind us. However, after a few viewings with disinterested but pushy estate agents, we soon realised our budget wasn't going to get us what we wanted, and I'd started to get despondent that the move might not be the right thing for us. Becky, much to her credit, is always the optimist, and assured me we'd 'find somewhere we like', and while I didn't share her confidence at the time, as soon as we walked into this kitchen, we both knew we'd found a place we could make our home.

It's a large room, with a beautiful granite-topped kitchen occupying half the space, and a cosy den area making up the other. But the feature that brought the biggest smiles to our faces is the huge wall-to-wall glass sliding doors comprising the back wall. With the sun shining in, as it is now, the room felt like it could be the centre of everything that could be good in our lives again. There was a definite sense of positivity and progress. This would be our new home. This would be our new start.

Now, Becky stands at the kitchen counter with her back to

me and William sits in the den, cross-legged on the rug, engrossed in what the TV is telling him. He looks so little in the middle of the large space, and my heart melts with how much I love him. Turning back towards Becky, she's still unaware I'm here. I walk up behind her, kiss her warm neck and wrap my arms around her. I whisper into her perfect ear that I'm sorry and that I love her. I can feel her melt in my arms, and eventually she turns to face me, smiles and kisses me back. We hug, holding each other tightly and I nuzzle my nose into the curve of her elegant neck, taking in that smell that always made me feel safe.

Except none of that happened. Instead, it just played out in my head as I stood motionless in the doorway.

This time for real, I think, I walk over to her, and when I reach her, I wrap my arms around her as I'd imagined, but as I bend to kiss her neck, I notice she is on her laptop. Or was. She quickly closes the lid, but that is her only reaction to my approach. She stands rigidly. She doesn't melt into me. She's cold. Why isn't she turning to smile at me? Why isn't she kissing me? I rest my chin on her shoulder and stare at the top of her closed, stubborn-looking laptop. She shut that pretty quickly, didn't she? I only managed a quick glance at the Facebook logo at the top of the screen.

"What happened, Ollie?" she whispers. I can hear that she's trying to stay strong, like she always does. "I've never seen you behave that way. You scared me, and you scared the shit out of that boy."

Her voice begins to break, betraying the hard, unwelcoming stiffness of her body. She turns her head, looks at William, still fixated on the TV.

"I don't know. I panicked. I honestly thought he'd been really hurt. I reacted badly and I'm sorry, I really am."

"You reacted badly?" she says ironically. "Ollie, you overreacted hugely. It was an accident and he's perfectly fine. You looked like you were going to hit that boy."

Were? So I definitely didn't. I didn't think I did, but I can never be too sure. Something to work with at least.

"I was just trying to scare him. Teach him a lesson. That there are other people in this world that he needs to…"

"Look," Becky interrupts, sensing the empty bullshit ramping up, "I know you've had it hard with everything, and I know you're having a difficult time settling here, but you need to try, Ollie. We moved here for a reason, remember? You said you thought it would help you find closure from everything, but I don't see it happening. You can't hold on to this feeling forever, it's going to destroy you. It's going to destroy us!"

She lets that statement hang in the air, and I can't decide whether it's a worry, a threat, or a premonition.

"We talked about this before we moved down here. You need to let go of it, Ollie. You need to try, otherwise all of this is a waste of time," she says, waving her hands at the room around us.

"I am."

I'm not.

"But it's hard."

Too fucking hard.

"Try harder then! Remember, it wasn't your fault. If things are getting too much, talk to me. Please! We can get you some help again." Her eyes start to fill with tears. "Tell me what you're going through. Let me in. I'm worried for you."

"Becky, I'm fine," I lie. "I'm sorry for before, but I was just trying to protect William. That's all."

"By punching another child, Ollie?"

She realises she said that too loudly and looks to William to see if he's watching us. He's not. TV wins every time. "Ollie, I'm not overlooking how bad everything was, but it's been two years now. You have to move on. I can't understand why you can't."

This isn't going well for me. Taking my cue as if from a film director, I hold her face in my hands, look deeply into her beautiful, innocent eyes, and say, "I love you." Not a lie. I kiss her lips softly and pull back to enjoy her reaction. She pauses from a moment, looks back at me and wriggles out of my arms to join William on the rug. She didn't kiss me back. Bitch.

I look down and her laptop is there, teasing me. I glance at her to check she's not looking, and quietly lift up the lid. It's a photo of a group of people. Becky is one of them and I am to her right. I can tell from the outfit she's wearing, it was taken at our leaving party a few months ago. She looks so beautiful and elegant as she smiles directly into the camera. A smile that still intoxicates me. I'm not looking at the camera, oblivious to a photo being taken, but I do remember the man to her left, posing with her. His arm is around her and his fingers reappear from behind her, a bit too low down her hip. Matt from her work. I look again. It's definitely on her hip and not her waist. Where does the waist turn into her hip? Where should his hand be resting if it were a friendly hug rather than something more tender, more sexual, less incriminating? I'll fucking tell you, Matt, it shouldn't be there, you fucking smarmy prick.

I close the laptop and turn to look at my family sitting on the rug. William has his head in Becky's lap and she is lovingly running her fingers through his soft, fine hair. The sunlight beams through the large windows, illuminating them in a kind of saintly way.

Was her smile because of the camera, or because of his hand?

3

Monday comes and it's going to be one of those train rides in. I never really considered how the order of your local train station on the route into the city could have such an impact on your day. Well, my day anyway. It's a short, fairly pleasant walk to the station, but any semblance of a good mood is ruined when the train eventually pulls into the station. Judging from how busy the first few carriages are as they rush past, I can see it's standing room only again. I'm pissed off. I'm pissed off that we all keep paying for our tickets, whether we get a seat or not. I'm pissed off because we're beaten. They've beaten us. We have no choice. Why would they try to solve our problem by putting on more carriages or more trains at their expense, when the robotic plebs that get on these things every day just keep paying. Drones. Pissed off.

The train pulls to a stop in front of me, the doors open and I get on. At least some of the other passengers shuffle about to make space for another piece of human cattle to stand. The doors close, and I'm immediately struck by how warm it is in here. It's quite warm outside but with all these bodies, it's noticeably worse in here. I look down the carriage and one or two of the windows are open, but without air conditioning or even any fans, it looks like this is as good as it's going to get. There are probably more rules and regulations to ensure the comfort of getting sheep to their slaughterhouses, than there are getting us to ours.

The seconds go by and the train still hasn't moved off. The doors beep and open up again. Either the train driver has been decent enough to open them for a late passenger haring down the platform, or someone has been caught in the closing doors in another carriage. Maybe they're not squeezing into their space quickly enough. Hurry the fuck up. We've got our carriage in order. We're all in our spaces. Let's go!

Glancing around, and halfway down the carriage, I see a middle-aged woman putting on her makeup, warping and stretching her face in all conceivable directions, the small plastic-framed mirror in her hand excusing her from otherwise looking totally batshit crazy. There is the obligatory sleeping fat man a few seats further down, his bald, oily head flopped back onto the headrest behind him, and his mouth wide open. At some point, the lower part of his face should turn into his jawline and then into his neck, but on him that point is indiscernible, hidden by fat, drooping skin. His fat face, melting into his fat neck. He's so still and unhealthy looking, it wouldn't surprise me if he was actually dead. No, I can just about see his chest rising and falling under his creased jacket. Not dead. Not yet anyway. Give him a year or two.

The doors beep to a close yet again. I look next to the heart attack in waiting to see who his unfortunate travelling companion is next to him. A young girl, probably in her early twenties, eyes glued to the phone in her hand, trying to block out the real world around her. In fact, other than batshit crazy and the melted head, everyone else is glued to their phones, yet no one is talking. I read somewhere that we've now got many more phones on this planet than people. So how come no one is talking to anyone? How does that work?

The train jerks forward, sending a few of the unprepared stumbling into the people around them. I quickly grab an overhead handrail to keep me steady, but the person behind me obviously doesn't, and with a grunt that I assume was intended to be a real word (an apology?), he, and everyone else shuffles back into their allotted spaces.

A few minutes later and just as I feel we're getting going, the train pulls to a stop at another station. This is always inexplicable to me. Having stops so close together is bad enough, but knowing how busy the train is anyway, it's just ridiculous. I imagine a meeting room in a shitty grey building, in some anus of a town, full of men with greasy comb-overs, wearing washed out shirts, pilled pullovers and shit brown ties, agreeing with each other in nasally voices that 'we could easily squeeze more people on this train, let's put in another stop'. Shit brown ties or shit, brown ties? Both work. Regardless, the doors open and to the silent yet perceptible dismay of us all, there are two new people wanting to get on.

"Move down, please!" squawks one of the women, poking her head into the doorway. Fuck, I hate it when they're confident enough to start barking orders at a group of strangers. But, to her credit, and probably because we really are all sheep waiting for our next order, that's exactly what happens. We all shuffle this way and that, apologetically invading personal spaces, until we all collectively, yet wordlessly, agree that this is as good as we can do. The shuffling stops. We're happy, but they're obviously not fully satisfied with our efforts.

"Move down, please!" bellows the other, indignation oozing in the ironic way she says 'please'.

A second, less concerted effort of movement and reorganisation ensues, and just when I feel I've reached my peak of physical, and more importantly, emotional discomfort, we all stop again. I look back at the doors and it seems it was good enough this time, as they're on. However, now with no room to move, I realise my left arm is trapped, wedged between my body and the body of the man pushed up next to me. Fucking great. I'm going to spend more time touching up this stranger than I have with Becky since the playground... thing.

They're both on, and giving no heed to the amicable silence they've disrupted, the two women start talking loudly to each other, carrying on a conversation that must have started from before they graced us with their presence.

"Oh my God, I cannot believe how hammered you were though!"

Oh my god, I can't believe how fucking stupid you sound. Please shut up.

"I know," the other gasps, theatrically. "I drank so much. I had such a hangover, it's terrible."

The word 'terrible' takes an age to finish being said, yet her face doesn't portray any of the remorse her words are alluding to.

Their accent, seemingly to have appeared almost overnight, is one spoken by millions of young people across the southeast of Britain these days. I thought we had all our accents decided. When did we decide we needed another one? And one so fucking irritating to listen to.

"Did you see Montana, though?" she carries on with a new, conspiratorial tone.

What sort of a name is Montana? Woman? Man? Dog? Whatever, tell us about her... or him... it? What happened? Why am I interested?

"Oh my God, what a fucking slag! I can't believe her!"

Her then. But what happened? What did Montana do to make her a slag? I get the feeling I'm not the only one on this train furtively listening to this idiotic, yet captivating, conversation. No wonder reality TV has infiltrated our lives so much; it's weirdly interesting.

"I thought she was going out with Harley?"

Wait, what? Harley? Slow down. Backtrack a bit, who the fuck is Harley in this soap opera?

"I think they were just sleeping together. But what a bitch, hey?"

Probably.

Realising I shouldn't be giving a shit, I decide to stop listening. Letting go of the rail above me, I use my one free hand to pull my earphones out of my pocket, put them in one at a time and find some music on my phone to drown out their dribble for the remainder of this Dantean journey. My playlist randomly decides to start with the song that was mine and Becky's first dance. Of course it would.

The train pulls into its final stop, my stop, and it's only a short walk to my office from here. This bit I still quite enjoy. Before moving here, I'd visited London a few times as a tourist. Once with mum as a child, once with school and once with a few mates after I passed my driving test and the world became that little bit bigger for us. Even after a few months of walking this route Monday to Friday, I still enjoy the buzz of the place. The noise, the rushing around, the suited men and the glamorously dressed woman, hurrying to some important place somewhere. Double-decker red buses heading to a destination off of the Monopoly board. Cafes already full of people getting their venti skinny white mocha lattes with an almond shot before rushing to their office.

And then, after all the hustle and bustle, I'm here at mine. The lift door opens at my floor, and the vibrancy of the streets are replaced by the stark and painful silence of the office. The only thing I can hear is the tapping of keyboards as people reply to the inane emails sent to them with equally inane responses. Must keep the cycle going though, to show worth and all that. I take my jacket off, put it on the same coat hanger on the same coat stand near to my desk.

I sit down, turn on my computer and nod a silent good morning to Ahmad opposite. Ahmad is OK. We support the same football team, so we sometimes chat a bit about the weekend's matches, but apparently not today for some reason. He nods back, quietly.

4

The day goes by slowly and, as I switch off my computer, I wonder what I've really achieved in the last eight hours and forty-three minutes. Not a lot, but definitely as much as I achieved on Friday, and probably just as much as I'll achieve tomorrow when I have to do all this again. What's the point? Why do we all keep falling for this shit? We spend most of our waking lives sitting in a box we don't want to be in, doing something we don't want to do, to be given money to pay for a box we don't really want to live in, filled with shit we don't really need. If we all stopped playing their game, I'm sure we could work something better out. Start thinking outside our fucking boxes.

Ahmad has already left, so I have no one to nod a quiet goodbye to. I just grab my jacket and leave.

The city always feels different in the evening. There is, of course, still a rush of people frantically dashing to their trains and buses to take them home, but there is also that swelling, celebratory feeling of a day's work done. Or survived; one or the other. The breakfast cafes and coffee shops are now closed, replaced by bars and pubs as the masses of designer suits and pencil skirts now find themselves in need of numbing alcohol rather than an invigorating caffeine.

The streets between the glowing office blocks are lined with people holding beer and wine glasses enjoying the warmth of the evening, spilling out and standing in the approximate vicinity of the bar that served them. I look through the windows of a particularly large, obviously popular bar. It looks alive, overflowing with the movement of the bodies inside. Young and middle-aged alike, apparently free of cares, with their loosened ties, expensive heels and designer smiles. I can hear the muffled laughter and the party-like noise through the thick windows. Stood here, on the other side of the steamy glass looking in, I feel like a bystander, a spectator, an outsider. It's a strange sensation to be surrounded by so many people yet feel so alone. After-work drinks was never something we did back home. I wonder what they're all doing there now?

    I continue walking to the train station, leaving it all behind.

5
Twelve Years Earlier

I think I knew from the first night I met Becky that she was going to be very special. There was obviously the physical attraction that made me approach her in the first place, but something much deeper took root in me that night. Our conversation was so effortless and her laughter lit a fire inside of me. I was already under her spell, and I didn't want the night to end.

In the subsequent months together, I started to understand what all the love songs were about. I wanted to be with her every waking moment, and when I wasn't, I couldn't stop feverishly thinking about her. At work, I'd watch the clock, willing time to pass quickly so that I could leave and go to her. She was a drug to me.

After a few months together, she casually mentioned she would be going on a weekend spa break in the Cotswolds with her girlfriends. I remember feeling angry and hurt that she could choose to be apart from me. I couldn't fathom ever making that choice myself and I envied her friends for taking her away from me.

I knew I was being ridiculous, and when we were saying our goodbyes, I did my very best to hide the petulant toddler within me. I smiled, wished her a good time and while I did mean what I'd said, as I left her house that Thursday evening, a deep depression hit me. I realised that I couldn't think of any way to spend my weekend without her, such was the all-consuming effect she had on me. The days passed very slowly and I spent much of the time sitting morosely in front of the television or staring out of the window just thinking about her. That weekend was the first time in my life I felt like half of a person. The first time that I felt like there was a piece of me missing. I loved Becky so intensely and didn't want to contemplate my life without her.

Which is why I'm going to propose to her today.

We've been together a year and I've always known this day would happen. I've more or less been planning it from the very beginning. We went to the Lake District on our first weekend away together, where we had planned to go on long walks during the day and sit in front of an open fire in the night. In reality, it had poured with rain from the moment we arrived, and so we holed up in the beautiful little stone-walled cottage we had rented and in between making love, we watched the old DVDs we found in a dusty cupboard.

By lunchtime on the second day, a bit filmed out, Becky found an old puzzle nestling in the back of a small cupboard in the dining room, and we spent many hours over the subsequent days putting it together. Drinking cheap red wine, eating cheese and biscuits, feeding each other from a punnet of fresh raspberries, and talking about anything and everything we could think of. The puzzle was a painting: an elegant stone bridge spanning a shimmering lake. Assembling it together was the happiest time of my life so far.

The weekend was soon over, but it sparked a two-week long internet search for the exact location of that bridge. There were times I'd nearly given up looking, deciding that it may just have been a figment of the artist's imagination, but after many hours on the computer going through hundreds and hundreds of images from around the world, I finally found it. It was a real place, and that's where I would ask Becky to marry me today. That's why

I'm lying here, staring through the murky morning gloom at the ceiling of our New York hotel room.

A mixture of jet lag and nerves woke me from a fitful sleep, and though the clock on the bedside table says 4:13am, I know it would be futile to try to get back to sleep. I begin to play out the plans I've made for this day in my mind. The route to the park. The route to the bridge. The private champagne breakfast picnic that will be laid out on the grass by the lake, set up by the events company I've arranged it through. Then the dinner reservation in the famous restaurant she mentioned once in passing as a place she really wanted to go, and finally the late-night ice skating. It's going to be perfect.

I hope the ring fits. I'm sure it will. I had spent months looking for the perfect engagement ring for her. While most of the rings I saw were indeed stunning, none of them seemed good enough. None of them would do her justice. As time went on, I was getting more and more panicked about it, until I heard about a jeweller in the city that would design and make bespoke rings. It had cost a lot more than I could really afford, but I'd spent a whole afternoon working with a professional designer, painstakingly creating a beautifully intricate platinum setting, before agonising over the various diamonds that would adorn it. The weeks in between completing the design and actually seeing the final ring were filled with anxiety, but when I finally saw it, I knew straight away that it was perfect. A diamond ring good enough to match Becky's beauty.

She stirs awake next to me and breaks my daydream.

"What time is it?" she whispers.

"Just gone four."

She groans disconsolately, but leaning across with a sleepy smile, she kisses me tenderly. "Morning, you."

My heart skips.

"Morning. Would you like a cup of tea?" I ask, wanting to start the day as I mean it to continue, making her happy.

"That would be lovely," she sighs tiredly, touching my face with her bed-warmed hand.

I push back the sheets and walk naked through the dimly lit room towards the kettle on the sideboard. As I potter around the room, cracking the curtains slightly to let in some of the early dawn light, I catch her watching me intently. I do my best to suck my stomach in a bit without it looking like I am, and while I'm opening the little plastic milk containers, I spy her in the mirror in front of me. The soft light I had just let in is enough to allow me to see her eyes, intently fixed on my body. Her unruly bedhead hair makes her look very sexy, and gives her an even more beautiful and alluring look.

I walk back to the bed with both drinks in my hands, place them on the side table and jump into the welcoming cosiness under the thick duvet. Becky immediately rolls on top of me. Her naked, soft skin warms me, her face a few inches from mine, painted with a sultry smile.

"You've got such a lovely bum."

"We need to get your eyes checked, Missy," I say with a laugh, doing well to hide the swell of flattered pride within me.

"No, you really do," she says as she starts to place soft, quick kisses on my face and neck. "I could just look at it all day."

"Weirdo," I say with a grin. "So, what do you want to do today?"

She keeps kissing me. "This."

I smile.

"OK, after this?"

"Ollie," she says with a tone of fake admonishment. "This

time yesterday I didn't have a clue we were even coming to New York. I have no idea. It's your surprise, what do you want to do?"

I pretend to think deeply for a few seconds, trying to conceal the fact that I've spent the last few months meticulously planning just about every minute of the next few days. During all of this, her kisses continue tracing down my chest.

"Well, there's a nice park near here apparently. Maybe we could just go for a walk there before it gets too busy, then maybe find somewhere for breakfast. After that, let's just see what we fancy doing," I shrug nonchalantly. "See where the wind takes us."

"Sounds perfect," she smiles. Her tender, lingering kisses continue across my chest, moving slowly down my stomach and then even lower. "But first things first."

6

The week goes by, and nothing much out of the ordinary happens. Nothing to suggest any improvement in things anyway. Everything with Becky is still strained and, when the doors to the office lift open, the silence that has been haunting me at home looks to have followed me here again. The office is empty and dark. Still, it's Friday, so hopefully the weekend will give us a chance to get things back on track. I've never come into work this early before, but with the important all-day meeting today, I needed to get in to go through my presentation a few more times. This is the first time since I joined that I've been invited to one of these reviews, and from the moment I was asked to present at it, a nervous edge has infiltrated me.

Silence seems to be a theme this morning. I woke two hours before my alarm was due to go off, and with my mind unable to turn itself off from what was coming my way today, I gave up trying to fall back to sleep and pushed back the sheets. Ready to go, I poked my head into William's bedroom. The glow from his night light illuminated his sleeping form. I found myself creeping silently into his room to kneel beside his bed and watch him sleep. He seemed so peaceful. Looking at him and listening to his soft breathing, I thought about the moment he was placed into my arms for this first time as a new-born. At the time, I remember worrying because I didn't feel this huge outpouring of love for him, but over the weeks and months, the love grew in me beyond anything I could have predicted. Looking at him in his bed this morning, I wondered what he was dreaming of.

I hadn't realised I was crying, but the tickle of a solitary tear down my cheek brought me back to the moment. I wiped my eyes, leaned over to kiss his cheek, and as I did, under my hand I felt the plastic sword by his side in the bed. We'd bought it a few weeks ago for his part in his first school play, and it was then that a gut-wrenching feeling washed over me as I realised that's today. I couldn't believe I had forgotten. At dinner last night, when I told Becky about my meeting today and having to go in early and that I'd likely be home late, William would have then known I wasn't going to be there to watch him. Yet he didn't say anything. It's no wonder he was so uncharacteristically subdued when I bathed him before bed. A wave of guilt and sadness crushed my chest and I had to breathe in deeply to fight the flow of fresh tears away.

Back to the present, I try to push these thoughts to the back of my mind as I make my way through the lonely office to the small kitchen at the back. I need to get a coffee in before I start my work. However, try as I might to think of other things, the guilt and sadness overwhelm me and the tears threaten to fill my eyes again. As I walk across the long, open-plan floor to the door at the end, the movement sensors turn on the fluorescent lighting, section by section above me, underlining my loneliness in this usually busy room.

I turn into the doorway and the shocked squeal I'm met with makes me yelp out in surprise.

"Jesus! I didn't hear you coming!" she says, putting her hand theatrically to her chest as if to calm her thumping heart.

"I'm sorry," I say. "I thought I was the only one here."

I've noticed her around the office before. Understandably. She's blessed with a girl-next-door prettiness and her youthful freshness stands out, heavily juxtaposed from the vast majority of us here. The world isn't beating her. Not yet at least.

"You're the new guy, aren't you? Oliver, isn't it?"

She knows my name.

"No, well yes, sort of," I stutter.

"You're sort of called Oliver?" she says, laughing.

"No, I mean yes. I am Oliver, definitely," starting to gather my composure. "But I'm not sure I'm the new guy any more as such. I've been here three months or so now."

"Well, you're the new guy as far as I'm concerned," she says, patting my chest as she walked past me to the fridge. Do I sense a twinge of coquettishness in her tone? Is she flirting with me?

"I'm sorry, I don't know your name."

"Keira," she replies quickly, holding her hand out for me to shake.

Keira? Better than Montana, isn't it? Keira. Yes, it's definitely better. Much better in fact. It sounds musical when I say it in my head. I take her hand and notice how soft her skin feels.

"Nice to meet you, Keira." The tears that threatened to conquer me just a few seconds ago seem to have been vanquished by this woman's infectious smile. I'm not crying, I'm smiling. Makes a change.

"You're the silent type, aren't you? I don't think I've seen you talk since you've been here."

Her tone is playful, her expression teasingly grumpy. I laugh and it resonates deep within me that she's actually noticed me before. More than once, by the sound of it.

"Am I? I don't think so. Maybe at work I am," I say, trying to excuse my behaviour to this stranger who seemingly demands constant enthusiasm around her. "I mean, I'm different at work. This place makes me different, I guess."

She sighs heavily, "Yeah, this place seems quite unique to say the least. It can sap it right out of you. The last place I worked was more like being in a pub all the time. It was loads of fun. Not much work got done, mind you, but people got on well. Some of them a bit too much, if you get my drift." Her butter-wouldn't-melt smile is replaced by a suggestive smirk and an overly exaggerated wink.

I get her drift. I very much get her drift, and I hope that my instinct is right and that she is insinuating something about her hopes with me.

"Shame this place isn't more like that," she continues.

My heart skips. OK, she's definitely flirting. I know it's been a while since a woman flirted with me, but this is a bit obvious, even to me. It feels nice.

"It would make coming to work a bit more enjoyable," I agreed.

"Yeah. Yeah, it would," quieter now. I can almost hear the cogs in her brain whirring over in thought. Thoughts of me? I hope so. "Anyway, new guy," the smile is back. "I'm glad we met, but the boss will be here any minute and I've got to get things ready for her. Catch you around, OK?" she says, disappearing out through the door.

"Not if I don't catch you first."

What the fuck, Ollie! 'Not if I don't catch you first.' God, I hope she didn't hear me. You may as well have said 'By the way, I'm middle-aged and completely out of touch, if you hadn't noticed'. Dick.

I watch the watery coffee drizzle from the machine into the plastic cup and I feel energised by my conversation with Keira. It's been a while since anyone showed any interest in me like she just did, and I guess I forgot what it feels like. It makes me feel, I don't know, different.

7

The meeting, and my presentation, wasn't actually that bad. Certainly nothing exciting happened that warrants a mention. The time seemed to go pretty quickly, which is always a good thing, and at 6.30, it was long overdue time to go home. I did think of William earlier when his play was due to start. I imagined him standing on the stage with the rest of his class, looking around, anxious and open-mouthed, for his mum. I imagined his angelic face lighting up when he found her, and a small, imperceptible wave of his hand to her as he glanced sideways to check his teacher wasn't watching him. I imagined him looking at the person next to his mum, hoping that it was me. I imagined him trying to hide his disappointment when he sees it isn't. Knowing he'll be asleep by the time I get home tonight, I vow to make it up to him and ask him about it all tomorrow at breakfast.

I'm walking towards the lift to take me away from the office and I catch myself scanning around for Keira. Not only that, I find I feel more disappointed than I should that she's not here.

I slowly trudge my route towards the train station with no urgency within me to get home. There's no point. With William in bed already, it'll just be Becky and me, and I can't handle the awkwardness between us. I know she wants me to open up about everything, but I don't need to. I'm not going back through all of that again. So, fuck her.

I wonder where Keira is now?

My eyes are drawn to the bar on my right. The same one that I stared into the other night. For some reason, it looks a lot quieter today. Maybe because it's a bit later in the evening, but it seems most of the after-work drinkers have already left. Having said that, it is still clearly vibrant enough with pockets of people scattered around. The muted hum of chatter, laughter and music makes its way through the windows and trickles into my ears. The dim lighting gives it a sense of seductive promise. Come in. Relax. Forget about everything, it says, casting its baited hook into my receptive mind.

I walk towards the door and I go in.

8

As soon as I'm through the door, I start to have second thoughts. My body twitches to turn and walk straight back out, but something in my mind overrides that impulse. Fighting the urge to flee, I snake through the crowd of people, making my way to the bar.

One of the barmen is already waiting for me and my order which takes me by surprise. Back home, I'd have been waiting a while to get served, the queues building due to the painfully slow, minimum wage staff who have probably just come from a full day of lectures or whatever. Amateurs. Not like these professionals. Waistcoats and pressed white shirts. A professional service for professional people. I've arrived.

"Good evening. What can I get for you?"

I fumble a decision, feeling flustered that I don't want to hold waistcoat up, and also because I don't want to look like an amateur myself.

"Just a beer, please. That one," I say, almost apologetically, pointing into the low-level fridge, at the group of green-labelled bottles I've never seen before. They look like they might be from a local micro-brewery and will show, I hope, that I'm different. Not just one of the plebs who will order a pint from one of the mass-produced household names on tap. No, not for me, thank you very much. I'm one of you. I belong here, fighting the conglomerates one consumer choice at a time. OK, so I've spent all day sitting in the bowels of one, but still. A worry gnaws at me as I wonder whether too many people now opt for the unknown brands these days, all scrambling around to be something other than what is expected. Maybe the discerning, confident drinker has gone back to the bigger brands, and they're actually the fashionable ones. Maybe people don't even drink beer any more! Fuck, this is a minefield.

I turn to look across the room, resting my back against the bar. When I first came in, I didn't really look up from the floor to notice how elegant this place actually is. Luxurious maroon velvet seating, mixed up with burgundy leather sofas scattered amongst the brushed brass and lavishly dim lighting that drips from the mahogany ceiling. There is a dark moodiness that the many flickering candles spread around futilely do their utmost to chase away.

The place is alive with conversation. Groups of men and women chatting about fuck knows what. Drinks flowing. Pinstripes and flawless skin. Carefree. Seemingly, anyway. I think of the shit going on between Becky and me, how it started in the park with that bloody kid. Well, it didn't start there I guess, but it certainly resurfaced. I wish I had smacked the little fucker now. Joking… I think. Why couldn't William have just seen the bike coming and stop? If he had, none of this would be happening. I'd probably be at home now, and not here.

Thinking of William makes me picture him, sound asleep in his bed with his plastic sword next to him. I feel a sadness start to grow, but it is ripped out from its roots by a nearby voice that breaks through the bustle of noise around me.

"Let me buy you that."

I turn towards the voice, then at my drink now placed on the bar, poured into a tall, elegant glass and resting on an opulent brass coaster. Back to the voice.

"No, that's OK. Thank you though."

"Come on, my friend, who turns down a free drink? You look like you need it anyway."

My friend?

The owner of the voice looks like he's exactly where he belongs. Exuding confidence, I immediately get the sense of an animal prowling comfortably in its natural habitat. A tiger in the long, yellow grass. Blink and you'll miss him, and before you know it, you'll be dead. He is undoubtedly a handsome man. Medium-length dark, wavy hair and blue grey eyes, strong jawline and angular cheekbones. A movie star. The sort of man you'd expect to see on a red carpet somewhere with a glamorous woman on his arm. But right now, he's on his own. No woman. No flash photography. Just him, and now me, I guess. Wait a minute. No woman and he's offering to buy me a drink.

All of these thoughts go through my head in a split second, but it's a split second enough for him to wonder whether I am second guessing his intentions. Which I am.

"Don't worry, macho man, I'm not gay," he laughs. "Anyway, if I was, I wouldn't be going for you. You're not my type."

The smile isn't out of place with everything else about him. Two rows of perfectly straight, white teeth beam back at me, his eyes sparkle with allure and intrigue. He's magnetic. Shit, maybe I am gay.

I smile back. It's hard not to. "Cheers to that," nodding my glass towards him and taking a long drink.

"I'm James. But friends call me Jay."

So, what do *I* call you?

"Oliver."

He smirks. "Oliver? You don't look like an Oliver to me. Olivers are weak little, *please sir can I have some more* things.

No, you're not an Oliver. You look stronger than an Oliver." He thinks for a second. "You're Joe."

Unsure whether I should be offended or flattered, I decide to shrug it off. Fuck it, I'll be Joe for tonight then, just keep talking to me. I take a long gulp of my beer, enjoying the pain of the carbonated burn at the back of my throat.

"So, what brings you in here today? Bad day at the office?"

"Something like that, I guess. I've walked past this place for a few months, but today, for some reason, I thought I'd stop in. I wasn't going anywhere else, really."

Why am I thinking about Keira?

"None of us are, Joe. Look around. In spite of what you may think, no one in here has anywhere else to go. If they did, they'd be there wouldn't they, not here?"

I take another drink and consider what he said. He might be right. I'd assumed everyone was here because they'd already gone places before. That they'd arrived. Achieved. I hadn't considered that maybe they're all here because they haven't got anywhere else to be. No one to go to. Hiding from pain, or loneliness, or anger, or whatever shit is overshadowing their lives. I picture Becky sitting on her own on the sofa at home. I do have somewhere to go, yet I'm still here.

"That's profound, Jay." I'll go with Jay. "I suppose they could just be here because they're thirsty."

"And cheers to that," he laughs, raising his own glass to mine. He looks at me, and then over my shoulder. His eyes narrow and his perfect smile fades from his face. He cranes his neck and sits lower into his barstool. A tiger in the grass. I turn to see what has caught his attention. As I do, a face turns to me obviously reacting to my movement. Keira?

Except it's not Keira. This woman is quite a bit taller, and she definitely doesn't look like the girl next door. Her green, smoky eyes fix on mine and just as I'm about to apologise for daring to invade her elegant world, she smiles at me. Waistcoat places a cocktail of some sorts onto the bar in front of her.

"Let me buy you that," I say, noticing my voice has gone an octave or two deeper than normal, giving me the air of being a hell of a lot more confident than I am actually feeling. I do, however, feel different to the man that walked in here only five minutes ago. Can't quite say what it is, but it's definitely different. Maybe this is why everyone is here, to be a variant of the person they are out there, beyond these walls.

"That's very kind of you, thank you," she says with a smile. For a brief moment, I'm thrown. I don't know why, but I was expecting her to sound like Keira. She doesn't. Her voice is sultry and assured, and with just the slight hint of a foreign accent.

"Ah, you're not from round these parts?"

She laughs. What a beautiful laugh. "Well, actually I am. I've lived here for twelve years now, but you're right. Originally, I'm from Toronto. Canada."

Her voice is amazing.

"I know where Toronto is," I smile.

"Have you been?"

My immediate reaction is to tell her I have, but then I know I'll come unstuck pretty quickly when she starts the inevitable discussion of places I haven't visited.

"Well, actually, no I haven't."

I feel stupid. That knocked me out of my stride. A brief, excruciating silence ensues, and I'm half expecting her to thank me for the drink, turn and walk away out of my life.

"I'm Yasmine," she declares, breaking the silence just as it toyed with the edges of awkwardness. It occurs to me that people seem very keen to identify themselves quickly here. Maybe because the city is so crowded, people are overly eager to individualise themselves from the hoard. Maybe they want to try and chase away the illogical loneliness created from the vastness of people here, connecting with a stranger who is part of the absurd conspiracy. Or maybe it's just because they're polite.

I become acutely aware of the ring on my wedding finger weighing heavy on my hand, and indeed, my mind. I ball my fist and push it deeper and firmer into my trouser pocket. I hold out my other hand to shake hers.

"Yasmine. That's such a beautiful name." Smooth. "I'm Joe."

Yasmine turns to pick up her drink, and as she does, I glance over my shoulder at Jay who smiles back at me and gives me a knowing wink. I find myself winking back and casually slip off my wedding ring, leaving it to nestle in the dust of my trouser pocket. I do think of Becky and, I'd like to think to my credit, I feel awash with guilt. But I need this moment.

9

We've been sitting on our bar stools for hours now, talking about anything and everything. Hobbies (if she's not eating or drinking somewhere, then it seems she's doing Pilates), music, stories from our past, some at least, and jobs. I'm still not completely sure I understood what she told me she did for a living, but I'm not willing to ask again. I've had to delicately traverse the questions of family and why I'm living in London, trying to fill the holes in my story caused by my actual life with the new, fake life I'm constructing on the fly just for her. What's the term? Economical with the truth. That about covers it. Of course, me staying away from family means I can't ask questions about hers. I decide, given the consequences, that suits me just fine.

She makes me laugh. I mean, really laugh. Her sense of humour is so witty and dry and I love it. She is so refreshing and I'm completely captivated by her. At some point in the evening, she repositioned herself in her seat a little bit and when she had finished moving, her knee was kissing mine. Accident or intentional, I didn't care. I felt a bolt of desire crash through me at the touch, and I hoped she was aware of what impact she was having on me. I wondered whether I was having the same effect on her. I doubt it.

Waistcoat has kept our drinks fresh throughout the night, and although my head now feels foggy and heavy with the alcohol, she seems somehow completely unaffected.

"So, Joseph," the so-far playfulness immediately vanishing from her tone, her eyes focus onto mine like a hunter on its prey.

A look I've already seen before tonight. "Tell me something dark about yourself."

"Something dark about myself?" I say, with a tone of confusion. "What do you mean?"

"Something dark. A bad part of you. Like, what do you like that you shouldn't? What sort of stuff gets you going? Maybe a bad secret you keep hidden deep inside of you. You must have something that makes you interesting."

My face must be betraying me, because I don't know how to reply. I feel a tremble in my throat as I wonder whether I should tell her everything. How dark does she want to go?

"You know, like in bed, perhaps. Anything naughty? Anything particularly kinky?" she persists.

Feeling slightly relieved at the direction she's taken away from the terrible confession that is always in the back of my mind, I say, "I don't know. Nothing really dark, I guess." I can see from her reaction that I might be disappointing her with that, so I decide to stumble on.

"It depends what you mean by dark, I guess. What your levels are. Give me some examples?"

That's better, put it back on her and give myself time to make something up.

A deviously wry smile appears on her face, her dusky eyes dance with suggestiveness and sensuality. She arches her back, unsubtly (to me at least) pushing her breasts out towards me, and gently bites on her lower lip. Her eyes shift from side to side, scanning the nooks and crannies of her memory, as if looking for the right words to say. Or maybe she is deciding if I am the man she wants to say this to?

It could be the drink, it could be this place, with its candlelight glow on her face and neck, but I don't think I've ever seen anyone look so sexy before.

"Like rough sex. Choking. Spanking. That sort of thing," she says.

Well, I wasn't expecting that! Her eyes burn holes into mine, stoking the raging desire already within me. A thought flashes into my mind. She's naked, lying underneath me, her long legs wrapped around my waist, her eyes fixed on mine and wavering between carnal pleasure and a beautiful fear.

What would Joe say?

"Why don't we go back to yours and find out?"

10

I wake up slowly and become immediately conscious of a violent, deep pounding in my head that forces me to stay absolutely still and keep my eyes shut. Thump. Thump. My mouth is desert dry and sticky. Thump. Thump. I wince as each pulse feels like someone is knocking an ice pick into my brain with a sledgehammer. Thump. Thump. Try to ignore it. Thump. Thump. I start to realise how hot I am, wrapped tightly in this duvet, my skin prickling with beads of sweat. Thump. Thump. This is not good. Not good at all. Shit, I'm going to be sick!

Fighting all urges to keep them closed, I peel my eyes open. I can't focus on anything, everything is blurred. My forehead starts to dampen with sweat and I battle my body's instinct to retch. I quickly swing my legs out of bed, my headache excruciating. Thump. Thump. Thump. I wince in pain and with arms outstretched, I stumble towards the blurred outline of the toilet door, fighting to keep the contents of my stomach inside me, for an extra few necessary seconds. Panicked, I push the door, but it doesn't open. Thump. Thump. I blink a few times to try to focus my vision. This is a wardrobe door. I turn to my left and then to my right. Thump. Thump. I feel my stomach once again try to force its contents up my throat and out of my mouth, but I just about suppress it one more time. I see another door and I stumble towards it. This time it opens, and I'm relieved to see a toilet in front of me.

I throw my head into the bowl, grab the sides and watch as a stream of brown liquid pours from me into the water below.

Thump. Thump. My stomach heaves and expels more of the offending liquid from itself. Sweating profusely now, the smell makes me feel even worse and yet more of the contents of my stomach drop into the toilet. God take me now, please, let me die. My wet, sweaty body starts to shiver uncontrollably and I feel another wave of nausea rise in me. I open my mouth; my whole body convulses and strains as I wretch again, but there is nothing left in me.

Impossibly, my head now feels ten times worse than it did and as I spit out the long, stringy saliva gathering in my mouth, I'm acutely aware of the disgusting acidic taste left in there. I wipe my hand across my face, ignoring the gooey mess I'm spreading across my cheeks and I carefully stand, my knees shaking in protest under me. Fuck me, this is awful.

The dim morning light coming through the frosted window lights up the sink to my left. Hunched over, I turn on the tap and cup the ice-cold water to direct it into the cesspit that is my mouth, swishing and spitting it out, before greedily gulping it down to pacify my hellish thirst. I splash my clammy face with the water and it's by a long way the nicest feeling I've had so far today. Thump. Thump. I need pain killers. Urgently.

I straighten up and catch a glimpse of myself in the mirror in front of me. Fuck me, I look as terrible as I feel. I barely even look like me. I look like an older, oleaginous version of what was once me. I open the mirrored cabinet and strain my eyes in the gloom, looking for a box of something to take this pain away. I see a blue box of paracetamol, pop two tablets into the palm of my hand and swallow them down with the help of another big gulp of tap water. Better have another one; this is serious.

It's only now that I can really begin to take stock of my surroundings and try to demystify this situation. Where the fuck am I? I had realised I wasn't where I thought I was when I was trying to throw up in a wardrobe, but there was no way my brain was going to be receptive to working that problem out then. It had its priorities.

The bathroom I'm currently praying for death in is lavishly decorated with tasteful sand-coloured tiles, and a huge claw-footed bath sits in the centre, dominating the large room. In comparison to the tiny bathroom at home, with the bath full of plastic toys and spongey letters of the alphabet, I feel like I'm in a spa rather than an en-suite such is the elegance and size of this place.

I look back at my reflection in the mirror and am once again revolted with the grey and sagging face pitifully looking back at me. I know by now I'm at Yasmine's. I know dawn must be close and I also know that the panic gripping me now is because of the ominous shit-storm this is going to create with Becky. The thought makes me feel like I'm going to be sick again. I need to get home. Fast.

I sneak back into the bedroom, and I'm relieved to see Yasmine looks to still be fast asleep. Considering the disgusting guttural noises I've just barked out, I'm amazed I didn't wake her, but thank fuck I didn't. It's going to make this next part a lot less awkward. Thump. Thump.

I see my trousers twisted on the floor, one leg inside-out from the rush of taking them off last night. I pick them up. A sock. I see my boxer shorts discarded on an antique chaise longue, peeking out from under a lacy, black bra. I pick them up and, turning around, I see the other sock at the foot of the bed. I bend down to collect it which makes it feel like my brain has smashed against the inside of my skull. I feel like I'm going to be sick again, but I take a deep breath and remain focused on the job at hand.

Memories drop into my fuzzy mind. The bang of the front door slamming open and Yasmine pushing me against it. Her hand burrowing into the front of my trousers. Her kisses all over my face and neck. I leave the bedroom and sure enough, our previous night's route is mapped out by the remainder of our clothing, hurriedly and passionately discarded. I see her dress. My shirt. Her high heels resting across my scuffed shoes, as if in their own private embrace. And finally, the last piece of the jigsaw, my jacket.

I pat it down and I'm awash with relief to feel my wallet, mobile phone and house keys are still there. I look at the phone, dreading how many missed calls and texts I'll have received from Becky, but I'm amazed that there aren't any at all. It takes me a few seconds to work that out, but then I realise, it's 4am. Becky is probably asleep in our bed, assuming I've come home late or drunk, probably both, and that I decided to sleep in the spare room. If I can get home before she wakes, then maybe I can get out of this and put all of it behind me. Just an extremely wicked set of bad decisions.

I get dressed and again I'm immediately taken aback by the opulence of the space I'm in. An ornate living room leading into an open plan kitchen. Huge bunches of flowers are sporadically, but tastefully placed around the room. A large fireplace under a colossal mirror. If King Louis the whatever the number of France were to have a house in London, this would be what it would look like. What was it she said she did for a living again? No idea.

I walk back to the bedroom, and peer through the crack in the door to see if Yasmine is awake. She's either doing a magnificent job of pretending to be asleep or she is asleep. I suspect her embarrassment of ending up in her bed with someone like me is making her go with the tactic of 'ignore it and it'll go away'. I don't blame her. Still, I can't help but take one final appreciative look at her. With her back to me, one long, elegant, tanned leg draped on top of the duvet, her perfect, blonde hair splayed beautifully across her pillow and back. She looks a million dollars. Fitting, considering the quality of her house, she's probably worth a million dollars... doubtless more.

That sensual image now burned permanently into my mind, I turn and head back in the direction of the front door. My head still pounds and though the waves of nausea are lessening slightly, I still feel pretty fucking disgusting. I slowly and quietly open the heavy front door, step through it, and turn to even more slowly and quietly close it behind me. Just before the latch will lock the door shut for good, something stops me.

Time seems to stand still as my head buzzes with a mishmash of thoughts. I close my eyes and picture Yasmine from last night. Her grace. Her style. Her laugh. I picture the person I've just left behind in the sumptuous bedroom. I think of Becky in her towelled dressing gown, her bed-messy hair as she yawns her way into the kitchen to give me an unsentimental peck on my cheek. My heart melts. I find I'm smiling at her.

But still, something makes me push the door open and go back inside.

Back in the house, I glance around for what I'm searching for, but aside from her clothes on the floor, it is pristine. I walk past the expensive looking sofas and into the kitchen, with its dark granite worktops and aluminium appliances. My eye is immediately drawn to the colours on the fridge. About a dozen photographs are stuck to it showing various people, obviously strangers to me, and mostly all with alcoholic drinks in their hands backgrounded by nightclubs and beer gardens. One photo stands out from the rest. Yasmine is wearing a lime green bikini, halfway through performing a perfectly executed cartwheel on a white sandy beach somewhere abroad. Her toned stomach catches the golden sunlight, the feminine strength showing in her shoulder and arms. She looks like she's from another world. I guess she is as far as I'm concerned. I wonder for a moment who was behind the camera capturing that strikingly carefree moment.

I scan the other photos until I see her again. This time, she's obviously in a bar somewhere, and judging from the decorations behind her, it's Christmas time. She's wearing a cheap looking Father Christmas hat, yet she still somehow looks so stylish and sexy with it. She's looking directly at the camera with an expression of false shock in obvious response to the lips of a man kissing her cheek firmly. His arms pull her tightly into him.

Who the fuck are you?

I study him further, and even from the side profile with his nose squashed against the side of her face, I can see he's very good-looking. An ex maybe, or worse, a current boyfriend?

Even though I have no reason to believe it, I convince myself this was the person behind the lens who captured the cartwheel. I feel a wave of angry jealousy wash over me.

With fury rising in my throat and tightening my jaw, I see a mini whiteboard, magnetically attached to the side of the fridge. In bright blue marker pen, and surrounded by hand drawn red hearts, is written 'Live every moment as if no one is watching!!!' I consider this for a moment, staring at the words, and somehow, in the quiet gloom of the large room, I start to feel claustrophobic. With the meat of my balled fist, I wipe the words away and replace them with my phone number.

11
Five Years Earlier

I'm sitting on the sofa in our living room. The TV is on in the background, and I'm scanning through various travel agents' websites on my laptop. It'll be Becky's birthday soon, and I want to take her away for a long weekend somewhere.

I did initially consider going back to New York, but I figured that would be a special return and so probably best kept for a more meaningful celebration. Our 20th anniversary or her 40th birthday, that sort of thing. Plus, I was thinking we could go somewhere where we could mix a bit of a beach holiday with a city break.

Neither of us are the sort of person who can sit on a beach all day and so the hunt is on for somewhere not too close, but not too far either. Some place where the sun will be shining. Somewhere we can lie on the beach in the morning and then explore in the afternoon. Becky has had a tough few months at work with one thing or another and I want to surprise her with a break in the sun.

I hear the familiar creak of the loose sixth step as Becky comes downstairs and I quickly, but quietly, close the laptop and put it under a cushion, just before she walks into the living room. I pretend to have been watching TV, and cringe inwardly when I realise the screen currently has two plastically attractive, bikini-clad women chatting to each other, the current stars of yet another ridiculous reality TV show. I snap my head to look for the TV remote, but it's too late.

Becky sits next to me and I can sense something is wrong. Her face is a picture of nervous anticipation. I can tell by the redness in her eyes that she has been crying, and I'm worried about what is coming next.

"I wasn't watching this…" I begin to apologise.

"I'm pregnant."

She frowns, but smiles at the same time, her forehead creasing. For some reason, my head jerks back as if I've been slapped across the face. In some ways, I think I have. I feel the muscles in my face immediately lose their tension and my jaw involuntarily drops open.

"Say something… please," she pleads.

The side of my open mouth curls into what can only be described as the grin of a village idiot and all I can think of saying is "Are you sure?"

She brings a hand, previously hidden behind her back, and pinched between her fingers is a little white stick. I don't need to see any more and dazed, I place each of my hands on the side of her face before giving her a long kiss on her mouth. She begins to laugh, unable to wait for the kiss to end.

"Is it OK? Are you OK with it?"

"Becky, this is brilliant news! The best!"

"Oh, I'm so relieved!" she sighs. "I didn't know how you'd react. I mean, it's a big shock to me as well. I'm not sure what I feel!"

"When did you know?" I say, kissing her quickly again.

"Well, I was late last week so I bought a few tests yesterday. I did one last night and it came up positive, but I wanted to be sure, I guess. I barely slept a wink last night. I did another one just now, and it was positive again."

We stare at each other in disbelief and I see her eyes slowly fill with tears of joy, as if saying it out loud has made it real all of a sudden.

"I can't believe it," I say, unable to think of anything else to say, but knowing I probably should say something. My eyes are wide with wonder and my face plastered with the same stupid grin. "Becky, I'm going to be a dad!"

"And I'm going to be a mum," she laughs and we hug each other tightly. My heart is thumping with happiness, but with my head over her shoulder, my gaze is drawn to the bikinis on TV. I spot the remote control behind Becky and slowly move my hand down her back as lovingly and naturally as I can, I grab the remote and press the button to change the channel. Antiques Roadshow. Much better.

The weeks that follow are basically a blur. We decide not to tell anyone else until we have the all clear from the twelve-week scan, but there have been so many occasions where I've had to hold myself back from telling people, especially my mum. She could do with some good news. However, I'd promised Becky I wouldn't and even though I know just what this would mean to mum, I respect Becky's wishes.

Becky is being very cautious, trying hard not to get too carried away with the emotion until she's sure everything is going to be OK. The only real sign that we're expecting a baby is the pregnancy book that Becky bought online, and even then, I notice that she's very careful to hide it away in a drawer when she isn't reading it.

I've been the opposite. The bookmarks on my web browser, usually sports and news sites, have been replaced by chat groups for new and expecting fathers, baby names suggestions, and pregnancy health information. Like most men I guess, I have absolutely no idea what is going to happen through this first pregnancy, and even less about when the baby is finally with us. I feel excited but horribly unprepared, and the time spent on these sites has helped me get my head around this ticking bomb that is about to explode into our lives.

I was particularly taken by a website that focussed on the mental health of the dad, discussing a myriad of things I just hadn't ever considered. Dealing with losing childless friends because of your shifting priorities and the isolation that may bring. The heightened expectations of the father's role in today's modern world, and strangely, to me at least, the loss of sexual attraction to your partner. I'm sure this last one isn't going to be an issue. I love Becky so much, and I can't imagine not being attracted to her, such is the effect she has on me. However, it was all really eye-opening and I feel better knowing what changes might be around the corner for me.

I've also started to compile a list of names I like. I'd asked Becky if she had any particular names she was thinking of and her terse response made it very clear that she didn't want to start considering it yet. Something else to wait until after the twelve-week scan for.

She has let me spoil her a bit more than usual. I've stepped up and now cook almost every night for us to make sure Becky is eating as healthily as possible for her and the baby. I religiously follow the recipes of a pregnancy diet site I found on the web. I've started to rub her feet every night, because I read that it can help to flush out any negative chemicals in her body that might impact our unborn child. I'm sure she's noticed that I've been playing classical music during the day, following the advice from sites that it could improve the development of the baby's brain, but she hasn't let on. As with the foot rub, it is probably all rubbish, but I just feel that we should give this baby every possible opportunity in life and if classical music could help, then classical music will be played. I feel like I'd do just about anything for Becky and little William, if she's happy with that name. I'm quite sure it is going to be a boy.

Eventually the scan date comes and we're told our baby is perfectly healthy, much to our relief. I'm just so happy that we can start to embrace this pregnancy now, and begin to prepare ourselves for impending parenthood.

Becky relaxes into her pregnancy and revels in it, in fact. One of the articles I had read had said that some men feel an overwhelming surge of love for their partners during this time. I'm definitely one of those. I love her more than I ever thought was possible. I can't wait to meet our child and to be the best father and husband I can be.

12

The rustling leaves above me try their best to shade me from the bright sun as its light flickers through them, threatening to stir me from my snooze. I pull the straw hat down further over my face to block the brightness from my eyes. A warm wind gently brushes the hairs of my leg as it dangles slightly off the hammock. The distant sounds from the sea birds circling above me in the azure sky filter into my ears. I'm daydreaming about a woman cartwheeling in the powdery white sand before me, and then all of a sudden, I become aware of her presence next to me. Her hand gently rocks my shoulder, consorting with the sun in the battle for my attention. I turn my face away which only serves to intensify the pressure she puts on my arm. *Wake up.* I fight it, but a now familiar queasiness rises within me. *Wake up.* A battle of will commences between me and my gummy eyelids. I want to open them, but they don't seem to want to be opened.

Wake up, Daddy.

I'm awake. William's smiling face is inches from mine as I look back at him through stinging bleary eyes.

"Wake up, lazy bones," he giggles. "It's the weekend!"

The sickness I feel seems to provoke a slideshow of incoherent images in my mind. A naked woman on top of me. My hand tight across her throat. Her eyes full of excited panic. A leg wrapped over a quilt. A photograph. A taxi ride. A sunrise. Silently creeping into the spare bedroom. And now William. Beautiful, happy, wide-awake William.

I look behind him and see the ominous figure of Becky. I

blink to focus more and she looks pissed off to say the least. I've fucked up. I've fucked up completely.

"I made you a cup of tea," William announces with glee, "but Mummy wouldn't let me carry it."

Becky puts the mug down with an audible heaviness that I know is intended to illustrate just how pissed off she is. She doesn't need to; I'm well aware. I focus intently on the tea as it sloshes about in the mug. A small spillage of liquid breaks over the porcelain lip and trickles down its side, pooling on the bedside table. It doesn't escape my notice that the mug exclaims in bright red text 'Best Dad Ever,' a relic of last year's Fathers' Day from William.

Who chose that today? William, unaware and happy, or Becky, very aware and very fucking unhappy? An avalanche of guilt engulfs me.

"Thank you."

I wince a smile at Becky, understanding my priorities, oozing with faux appreciation and trying to hide the physical pain I'm feeling. Evidently, I need to brush up on my acting skills. She turns and sweeps angrily out of the room.

I look back at William who continues to be oblivious to what has just happened.

"Thank you, mate," My gratitude is genuine. At least I have one friend today. "What do you want to do today?" I say, knowing that if I'm going to start to patch things up with Becky, I've just got to knuckle down and get through today as the perfect dad and even more perfect husband. It's going to be a struggle.

William's eyes narrow and he looks at me, his puckered lips muting the contemplative humming sound he's making as the options fly through his head. Then suddenly, with a jump and a gasp, "Football! At the park!"

Oh, fuck.

"Are you sure you don't fancy the cinema maybe? We can get a big bag of sweets."

Please say yes. Please say yes. I elaborate the bribes. "Maybe a burger afterwards, or ice cream. Both if you're good!"

Don't do this to me, son.

"Nah. I love playing football with you!"

You're killing me. Possibly actually really killing me.

"OK. Your choice." I try to hide the miserable resignation in my voice.

"Yaaaay!" He runs out of the room, his little feet stomping and shaking the floor beneath him.

I close my eyes and lay my head tenderly back on the pillow.

13

Later, after a particularly long shower where I was especially careful to scrub away any remnants of last night's sex off of me, I make my way into the kitchen. William is sat cross-legged on the floor in front of his cartoons, already dressed in his England football shirt, shorts and socks that he was given from my mum before we left. Becky is sitting at the breakfast bar, clutching a coffee for its reassuring warmth, her iPad, a black mirror, on the worktop beside her.

Photos of Matt again? I decide it's probably best to leave the accusations for another day.

"Morning," I say with a faint smile.

"What the *fuck* happened to you? Why didn't you come back from work last night?"

Very pissed off! Tread carefully.

"I know, I'm sorry." Be elusive with the response. Detailed, but not too detailed. "The presentation at work went well and I went for what was going to be a quick beer with Ahmad, and then one thing led to another. It was wrong of me, and I'm very sorry."

Ahmad?

"And you couldn't call? Tell me you were alive at least!" she hisses, glancing towards William.

Does Ahmad even drink?

"I just didn't think," I say meekly. "I'm really sorry."

"And what fucking time did you crawl in this morning?" The questions come thick and fast, smothered in accusatory tones.

OK, this is tricky. Don't admit to 5am. Gamble. Not too

early, not too late. What's right?

"I got to the station just as the last train left, so that would have been just before midnight. By the time I found a taxi and got back it was probably around 1am."

The dice is rolled.

Her tense shoulders slump a little.

"Hmm. You reek of booze."

Did her voice soften a bit there? Shit, it's working.

"I'm sorry. I really am. You said to try harder here and I guess I just took it a bit too far. I was just glad to have a friend, to be honest." Lay it on.

"Ollie." God, I love hearing her say my name, even now. "I just wish you'd have called or messaged. I wouldn't have minded that much. But instead, I don't hear from you."

She's still pissed off. Don't think this is won... yet.

"I figured you were probably drunk somewhere, but I was so worried. It took me ages to get to sleep, and even then, I didn't sleep well at all."

I stare at her, deciding it's probably best to say nothing at all. Let her talk herself around.

"I'm glad you've found a friend, but please show a bit more consideration for me next time please."

Next time? It worked!

"Sweetheart, you're right. I'm sorry. I'll let you know next time." I carry on quickly, not giving her the time to respond. "I tell you what, as you've had a bad night, let me take William out for the day. You stay here, have a bath, go shopping, or whatever you want to do. We'll have a takeaway tonight, all of us, put a film on or something."

"Too bloody right you're having him for the day," she says, her anger still there, but calmed and embellished with a slight hint of humour. "And I hope you bloody suffer today."

A wicked smirk forms across her face.

I can't help but laugh. She really is amazing. I don't deserve this woman.

"Becky, I love you," I say, stepping towards her and putting my arms out to her.

She playfully fights off my attempts to hug her, childishly, but fruitlessly slapping me away.

"Get off me, you drunk," she shrieks with a laugh.

I hug her, kissing her quickly and repeatedly on her neck. I feel her soft skin on my lips as her playful cries echo around the room.

"Daddy's drunk!" William giggles.

We both turn to look at him. He's obviously been watching us since Becky screamed a second ago and he's beaming with delight at seeing the, apparently, loving scene between the two most important people in his world. I turn back to Becky, her face alive with happiness.

"I really love you, you know," I whisper.

14

A couple of hours later, after another few failed attempts to cajole him to a nice quiet and dark cinema, William and I arrive at the park. It's another warm and sunny day, which I suppose I would appreciate most of the time, but not so much today. Even from just the short walk from the car park to the middle of the football pitch, I'm starting to sweat and it smells like alcohol. I listen to William, his football under his arm, as he details out the plans for the match.

"You're going to try and tackle me, but I'll spin and you can't get me and then I'll run back and you'll be another defender and you run next to me, but I'm too fast and…"

"Can we not just play and see what happens?" I interrupt.

"No, Daddy, we will, but first, you have to do what I say," he commands.

This obviously means a lot to him, so with a smile, I listen intently to how he wants to act out this sporting scene.

Maybe it's the sunshine, the fresh air or just being with William. Maybe it's all three together, but I think I'm starting to very slowly feel a bit more normal. Is that the right word? The effects of last night's drinking and lack of sleep seem to be granting me a reprieve. However, as we start playing, it's not long before I'm sitting on my backside, breathless and completely shattered, while William, full of his normal exuberance and excitement, pleads for me to get back up and play.

"You're just too fast for me, William!" I say, breathing heavily and wiping the sweat from my eyes with the back of my sleeve. William smiles with pride.

Just then, and much to my relief, he looks over my shoulder and sees a friend of his on the other side of the field. Just like the proverbial puppy off the lead, he sprints awkwardly towards him, football in his hands.

"Tom!" he shrieks. "Tom!"

Tom eventually hears William and runs just as awkwardly to greet him. They appear to swap a few words and immediately they start a game of passing and tackling.

The summery stillness of the day means I can hear their giggles and shouts and I watch, sweaty and exhausted. Fuck the cinema, this has helped, I think.

I think of Becky. I want to message her and tell her I love her. Tell her that I'm looking forward to spending time with her tonight. I really feel that way. Maybe it's the guilt. Maybe it doesn't really matter what it is. I pull out my phone from my back pocket and when I unlock it, I see a notification from a phone number I don't recognise. It must have beeped through when we were playing football. I open the message.

Hey handsome. You ran out on me!

My heart thuds in my chest. I glance up to check William is still playing and when I look back at my phone, three grey dots indicate that she is writing a message to me... right now!

You'd better not have another woman to be running home to!

This is the time to tell her everything. To admit to a series of titanic, colossal, arsehole mistakes. To apologise, blame it on the drink, block her number, and put it all behind me. I start to reply.

Ha ha. No, I just had to get somewhere,
and you just looked so peaceful, I didn't want to disturb you.
Sorry.

Fuck honesty then.

I know I should be feeling guilty, but I can't help but feel giddy and elated. I cannot believe this amazingly sexy woman took me back to her house. I can't believe she made me do those things to her. Or was it that she let me do the things I did to her? It's all still hazy, I can't quite remember.

I look at my last message. Beneath it, the word Delivered. Not Read. Delivered. I keep looking, willing the status to change, but it doesn't. It just stays there, goading me, as if saying 'You loser… she's sussed you out, prick.'

She's gone. No sooner has she filled me with excitement, than she tears it away. She was right there, and now she's left a dark emptiness in me.

"Daddy," pants a breathless William as he runs over to me, "I'm thirsty. Can we go and get a drink please?"

Sticking the phone in my pocket, I get up from the grass, take his hand and without a word, begin to walk back to the car.

15
Two Years Earlier

"Question number eight: how many bones does an adult human have?"

I look at Calum, whose perplexed face mirrors my own. How many bones does an adult human have? I raise my hands to the lamp behind me, trying to see if I can see through the skin and start counting.

"I haven't got a clue. You?"

"None," I say. "How many ribs do we have?"

Calum stands up, knocks the table, surprising me and everyone else in the pub, by lifting his t-shirt and sucking in his stomach as much as he can.

"Count them, quick," he whispers, holding his breath. "Don't let anyone else see!"

I laugh, but for some stupid reason, I start counting the undulations of bone.

"Done?" he asks, sitting down and taking a long drink from his beer.

"I think you had ten on each side, so twenty in total. Does that sound right?"

"I don't fucking know!" shouting at me through gritted teeth. "You're the one that counted!"

We've been coming to this pub quiz, on and off, for a couple of years now. I wouldn't say it was a regular event, but when we find ourselves in need of a good laugh and not wanting too much of a conversation, this is as good a place as any.

The very first time we came here was the day Becky gave birth to William. I was kicked out of the maternity ward for the night to allow Becky to get some rest after a fairly torrid labour, and even though I was exhausted myself, it just didn't feel right to go straight home. As I'd walked across the hospital car park, trying to remember where I'd parked in the mayhem of arriving shortly after her waters burst, I had called Calum to see if he fancied a beer.

He was always game for anything and keen to congratulate me in the proper way; he'd told me of a pub half way between the hospital and his house. I'd never been to it before, but that's where I met him, and it just so happened to be their weekly quiz night that night. We didn't take part that day, instead listening to the questions and guessing, badly, at some of the answers. The conversation was dedicated to the horrors of birth and my newly acquired fatherhood. Calum wasn't a dad himself, and judging from that chat, he was miles off being ready to be one.

"Do teeth count? Are they bones?"

"I guess so. They're bones, aren't they?"

Calum goes quiet, leans back in his chair with exaggerated casualness and turning his head slightly, tries to listen to the discussion going on at the table behind him. I don't know why he is so competitive about this quiz, but I love that he is. We've never come anywhere close to winning it in the past. In fact, our only realistic goal is to try to avoid the ignominy of finishing last. He obviously fails to eavesdrop any worthy intelligence and a few seconds later, leans forward again and quietly snarls at me, as if disgusted in me and my lack of knowledge of the human body.

"Fuck's sake Ol, you'd think we'd be better at this arsing thing by now! You're bloody useless!"

I couldn't help but laugh, which started him laughing and before long, we'd lost ourselves.

"Next question…," said the booming voice over the crackly speaker-system.

"Woah! Hang on! Ol, put something down quick!"

"What do you reckon? Hundred and fifty?" I ask, cluelessly.

"Do it," Calum responds, confidently.

"… country won the 1986 football World Cup?"

I wink at him, he winks back. We know this one. We both take a congratulatory mouthful of beer.

"Hey, some of the lads are playing golf Saturday morning. They're doing us a deal, fry up before the front nine, lunch and then the back nine. Fancy it?" he asks.

I frown at him disapprovingly.

"It's William's birthday party on Saturday, you clown. You're coming to that."

He winces. "Shit, I forgot. But I've paid the deposit for the golf already."

"Cal, come on. It's important to William. He loves you. And it's important to me too."

His shoulders slump and try as he might to hide the disappointment in his face, he fails.

"Of course, I'll be there. I'd just forgot, that's all."

"Good."

"Good," he nods assuredly.

"Question ten: which American author wrote The Great Gatsby?"

Cal rolls his eyes and shakes his head solemnly. I know I won't get any help from him, so I write down Steinbeck, him being the only old American writer I can think of.

"How old is he now?" he asks, cocking his head to one side,

trying to read my answer upside down.

"Who, Steinbeck?"

"Funny," he says dryly. "You know who."

"He'll be three."

"Three!" His eyes widen, and he looks to the ceiling with a face that is a mix of anger and bafflement, as if, like me, he's getting resentful of how quickly time seems to pass. Gone are the days when we'd be willing our next birthday to arrive, trying to rush headlong towards adulthood. "Christ, that went quick. Are you sure?"

"Yep, it does."

"Shouldn't you be thinking about giving him a little brother or sister?" he says with a conspiratorial smile.

"Well, watch this space."

"You're a glutton for punishment. Cheers!" He tips his glass to me and drains the last inch of beer.

I smile.

"Question eleven: what is the capital city of Djibouti?"

"Dji-who-ti?" he says, with the same look of confusion as before. "That's not a country, surely!"

"It's in Africa, you idiot!"

"Well, what's its capital?"

"I have no idea."

"Fuck it," he sighs. "Just put Djibouti City."

I do.

16

I'm glad it's Monday. Sounds a shitty thing to say, but being at home at the moment is emotionally exhausting. I feel like I'm walking on eggshells around Becky and as much as I love spending time with William, fuck me it's tiring. I'm sure I'm not the only person in the world to feel this way, relieved to go back to the office. It can sometimes feel like the lesser of two evils.

Though to get to the lesser evil I've got to get through purgatory first. Even if you had any happy, hopeful or positive feelings, the demons on this fucking train journey would yank them right out of you, eat them up and shit them out on the floor in front of you. They'd probably then rub your face in it, just because.

Standing room only again, I recognise some familiar faces. Batshit is doing her make-up and I can see what I think is the back of Melted Head's head. He's still not dead yet then. At the other end of the carriage, I can see the party girls, but thankfully, I can't hear them. Small mercies. I suspect they're reliving the latest pathetic gossip in their pathetic little lives. Kyle screwing Keeley, even though Keeley is going out with Kieron, and Keiron left with Kimberley. What's with the Ks?

I think of Yasmine, and it occurs to me that maybe I probably shouldn't judge the Ks. Am I as bad? Almost immediately, I decide I'm not.

Yasmine jumps into my mind and instantly, instinctively, I find my hand patting down my trouser pockets looking for my phone. It's not there. Inside jacket pockets, maybe? I squeeze my hand in and feel my wallet and travel card, but no phone. Shit! A panic starts to swell in me as I fumble through my bag. Shit, shit, shit! It's not there either. I'm thinking of all the things I'm going to have to replace. My bank cards are stored on it. I'm going to have to call the bank. In fact, all my apps are open, no passwords protecting any of them. Shit! By the time I get to work, there are going to be credit cards spoofed in my name, and I'm going to have debt collectors hounding me to pay for some thieving twat's new flatscreen TV.

Just as I'm wallowing in my own misery, it hits me that I could have left it at home. Fuckedy shit shit! Did I delete Yasmine's texts from yesterday? Would Becky, considering everything that is going on at the moment, go through my phone and find them? Maybe she already has! Fuck me, I'm in a whole heap of trouble. My heart sinks. An electric panic crackles through my veins. I close my eyes. Breathe in 1, 2, 3, 4 and out 1, 2, 3, 4. In 1, 2, 3, 4. I feel my head clearing. Out 1, 2, 3, 4. I lean against the handrail beside me, rest my head against it in despair and it's only then I feel something familiar in my jacket pocket pressing against my ribs. My relief is palpable, as I plunge my clammy hand into the pocket to find the familiar hard coolness of my phone.

I'll take that little glimpse into the atomic mess that would have been created if Becky had got her hands on my phone, and vow to myself to be more careful in the future. I'm fully aware that it's my actions, and not the contents of my phone, that are creating the chaos, but I mentally shake that thought process into oblivion where it should stay. Just look after that fucking phone, idiot! Maybe I'll change my password just in case.

I prod at the black screen and my heart jumps. A message notification from an unknown number. Although I'm fairly sure I know who the sender is.

17

I've had plenty of days when I'm struggling to get any level of motivation at work, but this is just ridiculous. I've been staring at my screen for what seems like hours, completely lost in thought. The last week or so has been full of thoughts of Yasmine. Yasmine with fridge man. Yasmine on the beach. Yasmine in bed, with another man's arm lazily draped over her toned stomach. Yasmine smiling at me, before her beautiful lips pucker seductively around the straw of her drink. One second her beautiful, soft hand is holding my own, the next it's holding someone's filthy cock as she guides it gratefully into her. I love her and I hate her.

I'm distracted from my internal conflict as my computer screen goes dark again. I quickly shake the mouse to revive it, hoping no one around me has noticed. I look, expecting chastising looks, but no one is paying me any attention whatsoever. They are all cocooned in their own worlds, headphones on, engrossed in what inane shit is on their screen.

I poke at my phone to see if a message has come through, but there's nothing. I unlock it anyway and go into my messages, just in case she's sent me one and my phone has decided not to work, but of course, she hasn't. I reread my last message for what seems like the hundredth time this morning.

Impressive! Hope you had a good night?

The question mark, you ignorant bitch. The question mark! Answer me!

Maybe her phone's battery died whilst she was replying. I

try to give her the benefit of the doubt, but I still can't swallow away this acrid taste in my mouth. I stare back at the spreadsheet on my screen, full of numbers that I just don't give two shades of shit about and then a vision flashes into my head. Kiera.

I grab my phone (you never know), and head to the kitchen, hoping to find her there. As I walk through the open plan office, I look around at everyone staring at their monitors. I think that maybe if I can try things with Keira, I'll forget about Yasmine and her toxicity. Bollocks to Yasmine, Keira is the one for me. She has to be.

A voice in my head says 'maybe you should forget about both of them and put your efforts back into Becky. I mean, she is your wife, you fuck-wit'. As quickly as the voice surfaces, I scold it away. Shut up.

She's not at her desk, so hopefully she will be in the kitchen again. I'm happy with that. It would be awkward having a conversation with her at her desk, with everyone else there to eavesdrop on us. Especially given the nature of the conversation I want to have with her. I step into the kitchen and the excitement that had built up is immediately extinguished. She's not here. I haven't seen or heard her all day. Maybe she's taken the day off. Shit, I hope she's not resigned or been sacked. That would be terrible. I'd never get to see her again.

I check my phone hoping there is something from Yasmine. Still nothing. I chastise myself. Really, though, what were you thinking, Ollie? That this girl was actually interested in you for more than just a fuck? She was probably regretting it while it was happening. I'll be one of her regrets, one of her personal lessons to herself, until she forgets all about me. Forgets what I look like. Forgets my name. Forgets I even happened. That I ever existed. Then she'll do it all again with someone else. Repeat to fade.

I turn to leave the kitchen and realise, for appearances, I should probably take a coffee back to my desk. I make my selection on the machine, wait for the brown plastic cup to fill and then head back to my desk, feeling bereft.

18

Kiera never did show up and after a day of basically being a well-paid computer keeper-awaker (who controls who?), I'm back on the street being carried along by the river of people streaming to wherever they're going. I decide to take a detour to avoid walking past the bar on my way to the station, but despite me actually choosing to do so, I still end up there. Fine. I resolve to ignore it when I get to it, to just keep walking past, but for some reason, my feet bring me to a stop right outside of it. The woman behind me bumps into me, unable to stop in time in the swell of humanity. I murmur an apology, but I can't quite make out her obviously pissed off reply.

I stand still for a while, staring through the misted-up windows, the boiling water of commuters rushing past me. She could be in there. But, even if she is, she's not invited you, so she obviously doesn't want to be with you. Save face, don't be a dick, go home. But Jay could be in there as well. But for some reason, even if he is, I don't feel I need him this evening. I take a step forward and re-join the current of people.

I get to the station, check the boards to see which platform my train home is at and trudge towards it. I find a seat and look around me at the other people. You never see the same faces going home, as you do coming in. Why is that?

I check my phone. There is still nothing from her, but I open my messages anyway, wanting to bring her back into my life just by putting her words in front of me.

Impressive! Hope you had a good night?

Not for the first time this week, I think fuck her. I don't need her. But, just as I'm trying to convince myself I don't, just when I'm about to give up hope completely, three grey dots appear. I watch them for a few seconds, unmoving, feeling frozen, and then a message comes through.

Hey you! Oh, what a loooooong day. I could really do with a drink right now.

A relief almost tidal in size washes over me. Everything is going to be OK. I love her. Don't dive in. There is a brief pause and then, to my relief, she's writing again.

Do you go to that place much?

No. Actually that was my first time.

Beginners luck then

For you, yes

I picture her smiling at that, hopefully even laughing. She's the sort that would appreciate the confidence. As long as she doesn't think I'm being arrogant. It's a fine line between the two.

Let's agree we both lucked out

Let's! I'd only gone for a quick drink, but I met Jay and then you came in

Jay?

You remember Jay. The man next to me. God's gift to women. The broad shoulders, perfect hair and even more perfect smile. Jay!

Jay... James? The guy I was with.

I'm sure you saw him.
You must remember him??

Eek. I don't. Was I that drunk?

She doesn't remember Jay? I'm not quite sure how to take this. There was a time that night where I had wondered whether she had only started talking to me to get to him. To get to the one you want via the ugly friend. Maybe she was and she's just being nice now. I am the uglier friend, there is no doubt about that. I press the thought away and read the next message.

So Joe, want to do it again some time?

Holy shit! I feel my heart thud in my chest and my head swims with breathless excitement. I do, I really do. Take a minute, Ollie, relax. What would Jay say?

No thanks. I mean, you're lovely, but I think I can do better

Instantaneously, she replies.

Oh, thank God. Me too, but I thought I had to ask.

I love her.

When?

19

Coco the Monkey stares at me with a look of excitable glee as he gives me the thumbs up from behind his bowl of cereal. His beaming face mirrors my own after my planning with Yasmine last night on the train home. His thumbs up, a sort of reassuring approval. I can hear his squeaky voice saying, "Yeah, we know this shit isn't good for you, but it's fun, so…" Thumbs up!

Behind Coco and the cereal box, William is devouring the contents of his own bowl, chocolate milk dribbling down his chin with each spoonful he sucks in. He's looking at the back of the cereal box intently, unwittingly absorbing the manipulative words and images carefully crafted by the marketing sharks, just trying to keep another generation of our kids hooked on sugary crap. 'So chocolatey, they even turn the milk brown!' As if that's a good thing. Still, we bought it for him, so we're just as complicit in the conspiracy as the sharks. Anything for a quieter life, I guess. 'So full of shite, they even turn the milk brown!' Doesn't have the same ring to it really. Quite ballsy if you think about it, hiding the problem in plain sight.

His eyes scan slowly across the box, taking it all in, as another spoonful goes into his mouth. He's completely oblivious to a stray brown rice pop clinging on to his upper lip. I can't help but smile at him, and I lean over and flick it down and back into his bowl without him even flinching. I love him.

Behind me, Becky is putting William's lunchbox together. I turn in my seat to look at her, her back to me, as she spreads cream cheese on a slice of brown bread.

"A few of the guys from the office are going for some drinks after work tonight."

No response. She just continues spreading the cheese. Maybe that was a bit too casual a tone.

"Yes, and I know it's not great notice, but they asked me if I'd like to go." I leave that hanging there for a few seconds before I cautiously go on. "I'd like to…. you know."

She stops what she's doing, her shoulders visibly sag as she places the knife onto the countertop and sighs. Not good.

"Ollie, look," she says with an exasperated tone, "I know things are hard for you at the moment, but in case you hadn't noticed, they're also hard for me too."

I hadn't, so I remain silent. She turns to look at me.

"I don't know anyone here either. I say hello to the other mums outside the classroom. I try to chat, but they're so cliquey. They're just not interested. I hate it, it's just not like it was back home. I'm lonely too and you're going out a lot more these days. When do I get a chance to go out?" Her voice is close to breaking, but she fights back the emotion.

"You're right."

Well, she is, to be fair and I do feel bad, but I have to see Yasmine tonight, plain and simple.

"I'm being selfish, but I guess I'm just trying to get everything back to normal as quickly as I can. Well, as normal as it'll ever be."

"I know and I understand, Ollie, I really do. But we're meant to be a team and at the moment, I don't feel like you're here any more. Even when you are here, you're not really here."

"You're right. You're absolutely right. I'm sorry," I pause for dramatic effect. "I know. How about you and I go out next week? Dinner somewhere maybe."

She frowns. "And what about William? Who's going to look after him? We don't know anyone!"

I know. But it's the thought that counts. Isn't it? Keep going.

"We can use a baby-sitter service. A professional one. He'll be fine."

"I'm not leaving him alone with a stranger, Ollie, come on! You know what he's like with people he doesn't really know."

"They won't be a stranger. Anyway, it's up to you."

I can see her face soften. I'm seeing Yasmine tonight whatever happens here, but I know it's going to be a lot less painful for me if Becky agrees.

"I tell you what, I know a few of the guys are married and some have kids. They're nice people, so I'll tell them we should arrange a couples' night soon. You can meet the wives, we can all go for dinner, some drinks. It'll be fun. We'll work out babysitters when we have to."

I smile at her as if I've just solved all of our problems and while the tension and worry in her eyes remains, she shakes her head in resignation.

"Just don't get drunk," she threatens, sardonically.

But still, it's a threat all the same.

20

I arrive early at Yasmine's lavish city centre house, and consider giving it an extra five minutes before I knock. From the size of the houses and the quality of cars parked outside of them, it's a very wealthy and quiet neighbourhood, so I briefly consider taking another loop around the block. However, I decide I'm far too excited to see her, so I knock. I can hear the clicking of her high heels on those expensive floor tiles getting louder and louder as she approaches the door. The light rhythm juxtaposes with the heavy thudding of my pounding heart. I become acutely aware of my clammy palms. Click, the door begins to swoop open.

And then there she is. My gaze is naturally and immediately drawn to her long-tanned legs, lengthened further by the incredibly short shift dress that finishes high up her sculpted thighs. The golden dress hugs the contours of her body until my eyes reach the light curls of her caramel blonde hair that rest on her exposed shoulders. And then finally, I get to her face, her beautiful face, adorned with a vibrant smile. Breath-taking. Quite literally in fact. I realise that over the weeks since I last saw her, I'd forgotten just how she looks. I'm shaken by the fact that she looks even better than I remembered. I can't think of anything to say.

"You can close your mouth, Joseph, it's very unbecoming," she says in a playfully dismissive tone, though I can tell she's flattered by my gobsmacked reaction.

We stop for drinks at a lavish cocktail bar, and the vodka martinis she ordered for me are already making my head swim.

I'm relieved when she suggests we walk from there to the nightclub, hoping the exercise and cool air will help clear the haziness in my head, but there's a large part of me disappointed that we aren't going straight back to her place to be alone. OK, so a just-about-averagely-sized part of me anyway.

While in the cocktail bar, I become very aware of the lingering stares she is drawing from both the men and women there. I feel a conflict between feeling immensely proud of being the man with this dazzling lady set against the rising anger within me when I catch men shamelessly ogling her. I just know they are undressing her in their dirty, perverted minds. Unfortunately, as we walk the short distance to the nightclub, it becomes evident that we haven't left those looks behind us. My anger turning to rage, I watch man after man after man slowly looking her up and down as they pass.

Finally, thankfully, I see the club across the road from us. The first thing I notice is the extremely long queue of bored-looking young people waiting to get in. There must be over a hundred people there, maybe more, and by the looks on their faces and their agitated manner, they've been there a while. Fuck that, I'm not queueing in that. Hopefully she'll decide we will just go back to hers.

Whether I faltered in my step or not, I'm not sure, but she must have sensed my reticence, because she grabs my hand, smiles at me and pulls me across the road. Without breaking stride, and definitely without giving the queue a second glance, she leads us past them all. She lets go of my hand and continues on while, for some reason, I stop dead in my tracks. To my surprise, or actually maybe not, she approaches one of the brutish doormen who sees her, returns her smile, and they hug. Of course they fucking do. They hug for a long, slightly inappropriate time and while I'm first drawn to the outline of Yasmine in her figure-hugging dress as she tip-toes to reach her arms around the man's vast shoulders, I'm equally drawn to the muscular and heavily tattooed arms that are now wrapped around her.

When they finally let each other go, I can't quite hear what he says to her, but she responds with a playful slap on the top of one of his enormous arms. This seems to make him laugh even more and he says something else, which makes her turn to point quickly at me before returning her attention back to him. He nods his head slightly and raises his eyebrows to me, which I take as some form of greeting and I find I meekly raise a cautious hand to acknowledge him. I shouldn't be here.

Just when I don't think I could feel any more intimidated and awkward, they both turn their backs to me and walk slowly away from the club doors. Try as I might, I can't see what is going on and I feel sick with jealousy as this display of intimate privacy carries on between them. Is he trying to steal her from me? Have they fucked before? As quick as I think it, my mind is filled with images of Yasmine beneath his massive frame, naked and writhing in pleasure as he fucks her with his undoubtably large… I can't even say it. My subconscious places me in the corner of her bedroom, tortuously watching all of this happen in front of my eyes. He looks at me as he pounds into her and when he starts laughing at me, my rage grows. I look down at my hand to see I'm holding a claw hammer. I look back at him, as the soundtrack of Yasmine's orgasmic panting gets louder and louder. The sound of his laughing distorts into a cruel cackle. I watch a bead of sweat drip slowly from the end of his nose. I watch in horror as it falls and falls and falls, as if in slow motion, until finally it splashes loudly onto one of Yasmine's erect nipples. The plopping sound it makes reverberates around the room, sounding more like it's been dropped into a long dark well.

The hammer suddenly feels weighty in my hand. I run towards him. A guttural, animalistic scream thunders from my snarling mouth. I raise the hammer over my head and swing it down hard into his face. Blood splatters. Teeth smash. Bones and cartilage crack loudly. I scream even more ferociously. It takes effort to prise the hammer out of his face, so deep did the first strike go.

A second blow, this time straight into his eye, which pops his eyeball immediately sending white ocular fluid squirting into my face. Yasmine's screams echo through my head. It doesn't stop me. He falls backwards, arms outstretched. The room turns black and Yasmine, the bed, the sounds, everything vanishes away in an instant. He lands, not on the bedroom floor, but in an infinite pool of shallow dark water. We're alone, just him and I. It sounds as if I'm underwater. Muffled. Calm. I hit him again and again and again. Each strike silent. His face pulps and mashes with each savage slug. I keep hitting him and then turn the hammer in my palm, hitting him with the claw, straight down into his open mouth, smashing more teeth and ripping his lower jaw from his face. His cheeks rip from the edges of his mouth to his ear lobes, exposing the stark white flesh beneath. I can see his fat, bloodied tongue as it snakes down his throat. I stop the attack, standing breathlessly over him as I watch him take his final few breaths.

The dampened sounds begin to clear and amplify, as if I'm swimming back to the surface of a deep lake and then, with a jolt, I'm back. I'm standing exactly where I was, the queue of people next to me, the noises of their chattering replacing the helpless gasps of breath that were just echoing in my mind. A motorbike whines past in the distance, the faint drum beat from inside of the club and Yasmine right in front of me.

"Earth to Joe! Come in, Joe." I focus on her eyes. "Are you OK? You look weird."

"Yeah," I say, trying to hide my confusion as reality washes back over me and I become more aware of my surroundings.

"Yeah, sorry, I think those martinis are hitting me," I lie.

Her concerned face breaks into a knowing smile.

"You're so cute," she says, scrunching her nose up, and actually pinching my cheek.

She grabs my hand and leads me towards the club door. As the doorman unclips the red velvet rope to allow us to step in, he sneers at me, and I hear a high-pitched scream in my head as his face flashes back to the bloodied and mashed meat I'd just created. His jaw hanging off. His eye socket black and empty. I sneer back and walk past him. Prick.

21

I follow Yasmine and step through the door. We are in a small room with a cloakroom and ticket booth to our right. The dulled thumping drumbeat from within the club is a little bit louder now, but there is still generally a feeling of the calm before the storm. I suppose I should be accustomed to it by now, but Yasmine is greeted by name by an attractive woman dressed in an elegant pinstripe suit, who ushers us past the ticket booth and towards the entrance. Of course we don't have to buy our entry.

As I pull the heavy door open, the booming sounds become crystal clear and the attack on my senses begins. The club is, as expected, very loud and extremely busy. The door shuts behind us, blocking any thoughts of escape I may have had. We are at the top of a short flight of stairs, elevated above the rest of the club, which gives us a panoramic view of the entirety of the place. It's much bigger on the inside than I thought it would be and even though it's very dark, the flashing deep blue lights expose the mass of bodies bouncing and gyrating to the music. We walk down the stairs into the throng of people and I'm immediately aware of the anonymity the sheer size of the crowd provides. It's so busy, no one is paying us any attention, all absorbed in their own world. A world that stretches only a few metres from themselves. Nothing beyond it exists. I can understand the appeal. This relaxes me immediately and in amongst the hundreds upon hundreds of people, I finally feel alone with Yasmine.

She grips my hand tightly and guides me through the crowd

towards the back of the vast room and one of the many bars that flank the room. As we get there, I see a good-looking, young barman look through the crowd of people baying for his attention and directly at Yasmine. He smiles and winks at her, giving her a subtle nod in recognition of the two fingers she has raised. It takes me a second but I realise she has just ordered drinks for us without saying a word or even queuing. God forbid, we have to wait for anything. She really does come across as though she owns the place. I wonder whether she's slept with him? She turns to me and her beauty launches a million butterflies in my stomach.

"Are you sure you're OK?" she shouts over the pulsing music.

"Yes, honestly, I'm fine. Just a bit tired, I guess. Are you sure you want to stay here?" I ask, with more than a hint of desperation in my voice.

She laughs, thinking I'm joking.

"It's great, isn't it? I come here quite a bit. I love it."

I don't necessarily agree, but I try to make a face that suggests I do and I nod like a cretin.

The drinks are put on the bar in front of us and she blows a theatrical kiss to the handsome bartender, who blows an even more theatrical one back. A small ripple of relief trickles through me at the realisation that he is gay. She hands me a glass of what looks like a couple of shots of whiskey with a splash of something else. I raise the glass to my lips, but before I can drink any of it, she touches my hand and gently pushes my arm back down, her face full of mischief. She leans in to kiss me and I let her. First a soft and lingering peck on the lips and then her hand combs into the back of my head and pushes me harder into her. She opens her mouth and I respond in the same way and as her tongue slips seductively into my mouth, it passes something to me. She moves back, smiling, and I can feel it's a small pill. Pinched between her thumb and forefinger is another tablet that she pops into her mouth and swallows it down with the contents of her glass. I'm still glowing at the touch of her lips on mine and barely give it a second thought as I take a mouthful of the warming liquor and gulp my own pill down.

"It'll make things more fun," she laughs into my ear.

I can feel her warm breath against my neck and goose-bumps prickle across my whole body. I'm sure she's right, but we'll see. I smile back, trying to appear unfazed by that fact that I've just taken the first illicit drug of my life.

We get another drink. And another. And probably another. Who knows? I like that the noise means we have to be very close to each other to be heard. I feel her breast brush against my arm as she talks to me. Maybe it's the pill, maybe it's the alcohol, maybe it's just being around this amazing woman, but I feel great. Really great. Relaxed. Happy… aroused. Even the shitty music doesn't seem as bad any more. I honestly couldn't say whether we've been here for five minutes or five hours.

I pull her to me and we dance closely together. Our bodies press hard against each other, her hands toy with mine, our fingers weaving together. The lights pulsate across her face. Blues, reds, greens. The music feels as if it's penetrating into my body and as we move together, I feel at one with this woman. I can smell the aroma of her perfume evaporating from her hot skin. She glows in front of me. Ethereal. I am in complete awe of her and how she makes me feel. I am in love with this woman. Fuck me, drugs are great!

She looks at me, her lips slightly parted, exposing the tips of her perfect white teeth, her eyes bore into mine with the intensity of a hungry predator and she kisses me. Her kiss paralyses me, making the hundreds of people around us melt away into the dark recesses of the club, taking their noise and movement and colours with them. It feels like the world has stopped turning and we are standing on this planet together, alone. I kiss her back, wrap my arms around her and pull her into me again. She responds by clutching my face tightly with both of her hands, gripping my damp hair and kissing me with such passion that I feel myself harden. I know she can feel it against her. She leans back, looks at me, smiles her smile and takes my hand to lead me away from the dance floor.

The throb of the club returns, as I surface from the trance she has put me under. She guides me away from the crowds into what appears to be a dressing room of some kind. I step in tentatively and she closes the thick door behind us, dampening the music down to a dull and distant throb. Looking around, the walls are painted red and the room is dominated by a large mirror lined with bright lights. In front of it, a sturdy table, on which are a few plastic baskets holding various make ups and brushes. I hear a click behind me which I assume is the door's lock.

I turn and look at Yasmine who is now a few feet away from me. She walks seductively across the room, looking at me over her shoulder. She perches herself on the table, hitches her short skirt higher up her toned thighs, and slowly, tantalisingly, parts her legs to reveal all of herself. My head is swimming with whatever drugs and alcohol I have in me and whilst I barely feel in control of my own body, I am very aware that what is in front of me right now is the most erotic vision I have ever seen.

I step towards her and I see her eyes are fixed on the bulge in my jeans. She bites her bottom lip as she quickly unfastens first my belt and then the buttons on my jeans, pulling them and my underwear down in one quick movement. I look down and watch her manicured hands grab at my erection which makes me gasp involuntarily. She pulls me towards her and I slide into her tight wetness with ease. A deep, satisfying moan spills from her mouth as I push myself as far into her as I can. I grab her hips firmly and I begin to thrust in and out of her. I cannot believe just how sexy she looks and feels. I cannot believe this is happening to me.

I keep pressing into her. She lies back onto the table to allow me to penetrate deeper into her and as she lowers herself, she reveals the mirror behind and it is then, in place of my reflection, I see the grinning face of Coco the Monkey.

Fuck you, Coco.

"What did you say?" she pants breathlessly at me.

I can't help but laugh a little, but I say nothing and carry on with what I was doing.

22

The hangover I was expecting the morning after the night before with Yasmine, luckily, didn't really materialise. Becky, to her credit, had been caring enough to leave me to lie in bed for a few extra hours after William had first woken us and by the time I was walking downstairs just before 10 o'clock, I was feeling pretty OK considering.

I could hear the murmurings of the TV as I walked down the hallway towards the closed kitchen door and, walking in, I saw Becky and William curled up together on the sofa watching Toy Story. The weather outside was glorious and Becky had opened the large sliding doors which had the effect of bringing the garden, and the sunshine, right into the room. The sun was already warm and coupled with the familiar smells of fresh coffee and Becky's perfume, I was awash with positivity.

"Morning, you two," I say to them cheerily, as I bent down over the back of the sofa to give them each a kiss on the tops of their heads.

"Hey, you," says Becky. "Good night? How's the head?"

"Not bad thanks, on both counts actually. I didn't drink that much, but I didn't have any dinner, so I think that made me feel a bit more drunk than I should have been."

"Good. Well, there is some leftover bacon keeping warm in the oven for you. Fresh bread in the cupboard."

I walk around the sofa and kneel down in front of her. I lift her chin, and I kiss her softly on the mouth. She is amazing.

"Thank you. I love you," I say, and I mean it wholeheartedly.

She closes her eyes, takes a deep breath in and sighs contentedly.

"I've missed you telling me that."

"Well, I do. Very much." I still mean it.

I give William, who is still completely oblivious to my presence at all, another kiss on his head, stand up and walk into the kitchen area. I open the oven, and take out the plate of bacon, dropping it loudly on the countertop as the heat from the plate starts to burn my fingertips. I open the cupboard, take out the loaf of bread and slice two pieces from it. I make the sandwich and as I take a bite, I put a coffee pod in the machine and press the button. Whilst the machine noisily does what it does, I turn back to the den area to watch Woody wave out of a window with Buzz Lightyear's dismembered arm.

Coffee ready, I pick it up with my plate and walk to the sofa. Becky moves her legs, curled up under her, to allow me to sit down and I finish my breakfast with my family. The sun shines through the window onto us all and the gentle warming sends a swell of relaxed serenity across my chest. I put the empty plate on the floor and pick up Becky's feet and rest them on my lap. I usually hate people's feet. I think it's the rough skin that I don't like, but I am always surprised just how nice Becky's are. I used to quite enjoy giving her a foot rub and without a second thought, I begin pressing my thumb firmly into the soft skin on the balls of her feet. I glance over to her and whilst she is still watching the TV, her face softens with a smile.

On the TV, Sid, the sociopathic kid, is currently getting his nasty surprise as the toys come to life, and when the mechanical spider with the decapitated doll's face appears on the screen, William stiffens and looks away. It's only then that he finally notices I'm there. Wordlessly, he moves himself away from

Becky and nestles himself under my arm, hugging his own knees. I know he's scared right now, but a wave of love crashes over me at the feeling of him squeezing his little body against mine in search of comfort and protection. He's such a beautiful child and I'm proud of each and every little thing he does. I wrap my arm around his frail shoulders and pull him reassuringly closer to me. I glance at Becky who smiles at him and then at me and for a wonderful moment, I'm exactly where I belong.

23

When the film eventually ends, William immediately jumps up, ready for what's next in his day.

"Shall we watch the next one?"

"Oh no, William," his mum says, "let's not watch another film now. Tonight maybe."

His little face drops and his shoulders sag.

"I've got an idea, matey. It's a nice day out, go and find the water pistols and we'll shoot each other in the garden," I say.

"Yaaaay!" he screams, as he runs from the room to find them.

Becky moves to sit and straddle me, spreading her legs across my lap, wrapping her arms around my shoulders and giving me a soft, loving kiss.

"I love you, Ollie," she says with a look of total sincerity.

"I know," I say with a cheeky grin.

The 'I know' response is just something we've said to each other over the years. I don't know when or where it started, but it always makes us smile and the implication of reciprocated love is not lost on either of us. She knows it means 'I love you too'.

"If you're going to come back in such a nice mood after a few drinks with those friends, you should go out more often."

I know she means it as a joke, but it still registers in the recesses of my mind to be used at a later date.

"It really helps. The whole night, I didn't once think about…" I falter with my words. "Well… you know."

"Good. I'm glad."

She kisses me again, just a little softer and a little more tenderly. She gyrates ever so slightly in my lap, pushing herself harder on to me.

"Judging from what's happening down there, every bit of you seems happy this morning," she says, raising an eyebrow.

I kiss her but we're quickly interrupted as William bounds back into the room and sees us both.

"Uuuur gross!" he shouts, totally disgusted, making pretend vomiting sounds.

Becky looks over my shoulder at him and barks at him jokingly.

"Quiet you!"

She looks back at me, her face full of lust, her eyes narrowed with desire and leaning forward to hide her hand from William, she places it on my groin and whispers seductively into my ear.

"And I'll see you and him later."

24
Two Years Earlier

Well, at least we didn't finish last. Near enough, but not quite last. The wooden spoon went to the cackling group of middle-aged women sat behind us, obviously using tonight to escape the monotonous drudge of their child-caring and husband-caring lives. They were quite happy with their position, seemingly finding joy in their collective ineptitude. Whereas our biggest laugh was the fact that Djibouti City really is, unbelievably, the capital of Djibouti.

By the time the quiz had finished, the marking completed and the winners rewarded, the crowd in the bar had dissipated quickly, leaving just a few of us who should have gone home hours ago. Yet we're still here, speeding headlong into a resentful, tired, hangover-destroyed day tomorrow. But we all seem to have drunk enough to not care. Tomorrow is another day to be worried about later.

Calum's eyes are heavy-lidded and his speech slurred and loud. I'd noticed that he'd finished his drinks a lot quicker than I had and I'd skipped a few rounds, so I'm not feeling anywhere near as drunk as he looks. I inwardly congratulate myself, knowing that while I'll be tired tomorrow, I can cope with that and the duties of doing my bit with William. Put a hangover into that mix and it's a whole different, agonising ball game.

"Hey, guess where Harry is going with his mates?" he slurs.

"Bogner?" I don't care.

"Shut up. No, Vietnam. Vietnam! What is happening to kids

these days?" he looks truly baffled. "What happened to finishing your A Levels, flying to some place in the Med, drinking your own bodyweight in ouzo and shagging girls on the beach?"

I can't help but laugh, as we both know that's exactly what happened on our first holiday together, minus the girls bit for me, unfortunately.

"Hey," he says quietly leaning in and lowering his voice. "Do you remember that German girl? I can't remember her name, but you know, she emailed me a few months after we got back."

"Why?"

"She told me she was pregnant," the open-mouthed shock on his face mimicking exactly how it would have looked the day he got the email. "She said it had to be mine."

"How could she have been so sure?" I say without thinking.

"She was a virgin," he says with a vile grin.

"You're disgusting, Cal, you know that?"

"Me? Why?" He gasps, pretending to grasp at a painful dagger in his heart.

"Did you know she was when you went to the beach?"

"No! Of course not. I'm not a fucking animal," he says, admonishing my harsh judgement of him. "She told me just before I put it in."

I shake my head.

"And you didn't think perhaps you should have done the right thing? Walk away and let her lose it in a more special way, to someone less of a prick than you? You know, like just about anyone else on this planet."

"God, you're such a pussy sometimes, you know that?"

His smile is so contagious, and it's moments like this I can see why he does so well with women. Just not the right sort of women, obviously.

"It was up to her. We're not all Mr. fucking Darcy romantic gobshites you know. It's just sex, no biggy."

I shake my head again. I hope I never have a daughter. I'd hate for her to grow up and meet a Calum.

"Anyway, so she tells me she's pregnant, it's mine, and she wants to have it. Can you fucking believe that?"

"How come you've never told me this before?"

"I don't know. I just thought about it now."

"So what happened?"

He looks at me with a devious smirk on his face and I can tell what's coming.

"No idea, I deleted the email," he laughs loudly and slaps the table loudly. "Fuck knows, my friend!"

The group of women behind us all turn their heads towards us and I look back and smile an apology at them.

"So for all you know," I say quietly to him, "you've got a kid running around somewhere. It'd be what, fifteen or sixteen now."

He appears to find this funny.

"Ha, yea! A little Hans or Gertrude! Imagine!" he shouts and then his smile vanishes to portray a more serious expression. "He'd be a good-looking thing though, obviously."

We both stare at each other for a brief moment before the laughter takes over us. Nothing about Calum surprises me any more, but I love him for it all the same.

"Anyway," he continues when we finally stop laughing, "it's not as if I was the only deviant on that holiday. We all have plenty to be ashamed of!"

"True," I admit. It was definitely a coming-of-age fortnight for all seven of us. I have lots of fond memories of that time.

"Do you remember Smithy that one night? Didn't he finish

a whole box of red wine?"

"And then a few cocktails and beers. He was a monster. He was so smashed," he laughs.

"Wasn't that the night you challenged him to bite his own nose?"

More laughter, tears filling our eyes at the recollection.

"He was rolling around on the floor for ages. 'It's getting away! It's getting away!' he was screaming," Calum shouts.

We are howling with laughter by now, wiping tears away from my cheeks with my sleeves.

"I miss this," I say, looking down at my feet.

"Fuck me, if I did a holiday like that now, I'd end up dead. My hangovers last most of the week these days."

"No, I don't mean that. I mean this. Us." He sags in front of me. "Before life got serious, you know?"

"Did it get serious?" he says with a faux look of astonishment. "No one told me."

I laugh. "Well, it did for some of us."

He reaches over and puts his hand on my hand, which I was resting on the table between us.

"Shall we just fuck and get it out of the way?"

"Piss off!" I say, snapping my hand back.

"What? Wait! Haven't we been flirting?" he says with confusion. "You bitch, you've been leading me on all night!"

"You'd only get me pregnant and then ignore my emails."

He stands, swallows the last dregs of beer in his glass and, swaying slightly, says with a flourish, "And on that rather homoerotic note, I think we should call it a night."

"Yeah, good idea," I say, standing up myself.

He fumbles in his jean pocket and pulls his car keys out.

"Mate, you're not driving in that state," I say firmly.

"I know. I was just hoping you'd join me in the backseat," he says, playfully grabbing for my crotch, which I jump back to avoid. "Come on, you little prick tease... not even just a little hand job?"

We laugh.

25

The office this Monday is, as usual, quiet, monotonous, insipid, worthless. As typical as that may be, surprisingly, I'm feeling very much the opposite. The weekend was great, from start to finish. William and I had a lot of quality time together, full of love and laughter. Water fights, football at the park (three times) and the highlight, finally getting the stabilisers off of his bike. There were a few falls and some tears over a scratched knee, but the sound of his laughter fills my head even now. He was so proud of himself, and I was too.

And of course, Becky.

Something seemed to change between us. The endless moody darkness hovering over us these last few years seemed to finally feel like a distant memory. The way we once were. I don't know, it was just… good. Better than good actually. Great. If you've ever been ill for a while, you begin to forget what it's like to feel normal. I'd forgotten what normal life felt like and I'm hoping this means it's the end of everything from before.

The last few days have reminded me about all the good things we have. The time with Becky was like it was when we were in the early, exciting days of our relationship. For the first time in a long time, we held hands when we were together. We hugged, not because it felt like we should, or because we were consoling each other, but because we wanted to. Because we needed to.

The sex that night, as was intimated by her good mood through the day, was great. Different to sex with Yasmine. In a good way. Becky knows me, knows what I like. She can play with my body and mind like a grandmaster on her piano. Whilst Yasmine is exquisite and the sex is exciting, it is… different. I feel that I'm more concerned with pleasing her. I wonder whether what I'm doing is working for her?

I can't help but compare myself with the men from her past and I never compare myself well, even though I have no reason to suggest otherwise. With Becky, it's comfortable. Habitual. In the past, I would have used those sorts of words negatively, dismissive of a routine sex life, but not now. Now, I see it for the good it brings. The familiar, the routine, that lightness of mind, I realise now, is the essence of what a love life should be.

I didn't need to hear Becky say it, but when she did say that she felt I was a different man (in a good way she added quickly), I knew what she meant. I knew I felt different for her. I feel different in myself. In spite of what has, and is, happening with Yasmine, somehow, I feel like a better husband to Becky with Yasmine in my life. It's strange to say it, but I felt myself rebound from my night of being Joe, to being a better Oliver. As long as it makes me feel this way, then surely, I'm justified to keep things going with Yasmine. Whatever Becky doesn't know doesn't hurt surely? And she's getting the best of me again. Whatever medicine helps. Right?

I even found that when I saw Becky on Facebook, I wasn't bothered by what she may or may not have been doing. I pictured Yasmine, lying in front of me on the table in the club, her sounds, her scent, and that helped me cope and deal with anything Becky and Facebook could throw at me. Yasmine is helping Becky and me. She is the breeze that has blown the ominous, dark clouds from our lives.

I'm meeting Yasmine for a late lunch this afternoon. We

messaged each other on my way in to work this morning and although I'm going to have to sneak out of the office early to see her, I don't care. Work can fuck off. What's the worst they can do to me? They're not stopping me. Not while this is all finally working out for me. Not now I've found my cure.

I look at the clock and it's almost time to leave to get to her. I check the tube map app on my phone for the sixth time today, reminding myself again of the route to Knightsbridge. It's not an area I go to often and it'll take me the best part of half an hour to get there.

With excitement fizzing through me, I stand to leave.

26

I arrive at the restaurant a few minutes early but my good mood has already been soured by the disapproving raised eyebrow the maître d' shot at me when I told him we had a booking under the name 'Yasmine'. I'm assuming Yasmine is a regular here and I'm already starting to think I'm probably just the next man she's brought here. Or maybe the daft old twat is, himself, in love with Yasmine. Maybe he's just jealous that I'm the man she chooses to sit at a table with and he's just the man to bring her to me. So fuck you.

It's a nice restaurant. The dark oak bar and matching tables and chairs would give a heaviness to the room if it wasn't for the large windows at the front that gives the whole place a bright, floaty ambience. They've obviously tried to make it feel like we're in a quintessential English garden and flicking through the menu in front of me, I can see it's more about traditional afternoon tea at this time of day. Orange Pekoe from Sri Lanka and Chinese Monkey Leaf. I feel a bit awkward in these decadent surrounds and the prices on the menu do nothing to comfort me.

I look around at my fellow guests here and notice it's predominately a mix of the ladies-that-lunch set and overweight American tourists, with their ill-fitting shiny jackets and gaudy baseball caps. There is a table of two twenty-something Chinese girls, both wearing oversized Burberry check trench coats, surrounded by huge shopping bags from Rigby and Peller, Harvey Nichols and Prada.

Their champagne glasses have been topped up from the

bottle of Ruinart Blanc de Blancs in the ice bucket next to them. They have had them in their hands for a few minutes now, but haven't managed to drink any of it yet. They are going through the seemingly obligatory, modern-day routine of documenting their whole lives through taking a myriad of contrived selfies.

I watch one of them with a contempt I can't really trace. I don't think I'll ever understand these types of people, hell bent on sharing their lives with complete strangers. If they realised just how shit they were making the majority of their followers feel, I'd like to think they'd have a sense of guilt. Or maybe that's one of the reasons they do it. A sort of socio-cyber bullying.

Just as I start to picture snatching the crystal glass from her grasp and smashing it into her smug young face, I see movement at the front desk. I turn and there, looking so perfect and elegant, I see Yasmine laughing at something with the maître d'.

Just do your job and bring her to me, you prick.

Sure enough, he does and as she gets closer, I stand to greet her. She pecks me on the lips with such familiarity that I can't help but look at him with as smug a 'fuck you' face as I can. In response, his face tightens and I know he would probably throw a punch at me if we weren't where we are. But we are. So fuck you. I win.

"Lucien, we'll have the afternoon tea for two, but could you bring the mignardises now, my blood sugar is a bit low," she says as she lowers herself into the plush green chair opposite me.

"Certainly, Ms. Irving, right away. Would *madame* like her usual white wine?"

Irving? Did I know that? I don't think I did. I think as I take my seat.

"Oh, yes please, Lucien, thank you," she smiles at him, but looks at me.

"Very good *madame*, a bottle of the 2002 Les Meurgers," he replies, bowing.

Prick.

Did he say 2002? A sudden mild panic settles in the pit of my stomach as I realise that I'm probably going to have to pay the bill for all of this. I try to surreptitiously scan the menu for the price tag on what she's just ordered, but well aware of what I'm doing, the prick Lucien snatches it from my hands. He sneers superciliously at me, bows to Yasmine and leaves.

Fuuuuuck youuuuu.

"Sorry I'm late, it's been a crazy afternoon," she sighs.

I say what I think. "You look beautiful."

Her shoulders visibly slump, and the tension in her face mellows. She smiles and reaches across the table to place her elegant hand on top of mine. I love that hand.

"Thank you, Joseph," she replies with sincerity.

"So, this is a little different to where we were the last time we saw each other," I smirk.

She cocks her head to one side. Is she trying to remember where we were last time? Has she forgotten about it already? She takes her hand off mine and leans back in the chair without a word. OK, that felt cold, didn't it?

A waiter arrives at our table with a plate of small cakes, the migna-whatever she said, and backs away to allow another waiter to present me with the bottle of wine she ordered. Shit, it does say '2002'. Sounds expensive. I nod in affirmation and go through the painful ritual of trying the proffered taster, before again nodding to indicate it has passed my not-so-discerning palate. He and I both know this was always going to be the way it played out, yet we still went through the motions. I've never turned a wine down at this point before. I make a mental note to do it next time, just to see what happens.

27

The time with Yasmine is perfect and while we're surrounded by the rather uncomfortable and stuffy pomp, the conversation is anything but. She is stunning and yet again I'm enjoying how she makes me feel. I make her laugh plenty of times as the various courses are brought to us and the room feels like our own. I turn to my right and realise I didn't even notice the Chinese couple leave.

"Well, this has been lovely, Joseph," she says, breaking the spell and bringing the time to an end as she stands. "Oh, my friend David is having a little house party at the end of the month. You should come."

End of the month!

I'm jarred by how quickly this is finishing. Have I bored her? Have I said something wrong? I don't think I have.

"Right, OK, yes, that sounds good." I'm reeling. "Are we not going to see each other before then?" I ask, trying to keep the sound of desperation out of my voice. I don't think I did though.

"I'd love to, Joseph, but I've got to go back to Canada tomorrow morning. A family thing. Don't worry about it."

"Oh. Right. When will you be back?" I know I sound pathetic, but I'm panicking.

"Not sure yet. A week or so. Not long."

She seems so dismissive, as if she doesn't appreciate the effect her absence will have on me. With no time to prepare, I have to go cold turkey on this magical woman. This cure.

At some point in the exchange, I have stood up and she

kisses me again on my lips, hugs me, and says into my ear, "I'll call you when I'm back, OK?"

Not really a question. I want to say 'no, no it's not fucking OK', because it isn't. You can't leave like this. Thankfully I'm too dumbstruck to verbalise anything.

I watch her leave, waiting pitifully for her to look back at me, but that look never comes. She says something to Lucien and sweeps out of the restaurant as quickly as she swept in, taking with her the light and life that follows her wherever she goes.

It feels like someone has pressed the play button to restart the rest of the world around me, paused while we were together. I sit.

Dejected.

Deflated.

Staring at her still half full glass of wine, a gentle smudge of her lipstick still on the rim of the crystal. A remnant of her. An echo. The only visible proof that she actually was here, gracing us all with her presence.

A waiter comes to the table to clear her plate and I ask for the bill.

"*Madame* has already paid, sir," he informs me.

Two thousand and two 'thank fucks for that'.

28

I walk slowly back to the underground station, aware that since Yasmine seemed to cut short our date, I would arrive home earlier than normal if I went back now. I can't go back to work, so for the time being at least, I don't belong anywhere. I'm in the no-man's land between my two lives.

I kill some time by wandering inanely in and out of various shops on the way, trying to avoid eye contact with any of the salespeople. It's amazing how time can go so quickly when you don't want it to, but it'll drag when you do. I feel that this is time wasted. Time I should be spending with Yasmine, but time that she has taken from me. These wasted minutes have robbed precious moments with her. Juxtaposing how shit this time is in comparison to how it would have been with her makes it all feel even worse.

I get to my underground station but I continue on, passing it, deciding to walk to the next one. When I get there, I'm still too early, so I keep going to the next. Why did she leave so early? So quickly?

Eventually, with my feet aching from the long walk, I head into the final underground station. I'm the only one in the melee that isn't rushing anywhere. I'm the outsider again, the pariah.

The long escalator takes me into the bowels of the underground system, and I watch the solid line of people pass me going up to street level. I spot a young, pretty woman about twenty feet below. As the machinery of the escalator brings us closer, I see her looks don't necessarily fulfil the promise suggested when I first saw her from a distance. But I still stare, hoping she'll look at me as she slowly goes past. She doesn't.

I get to the busy platform and decide to let everyone join the train that has just whooshed in. The board says the next one is due in two minutes and I figure I've got a better chance of a seat on it. Plus, it's not like I'm in a rush. I watch as people cram on, the doors clank shut, and the train accelerates away. For a few seconds, I'm alone on the long, quiet platform, and the unusual stillness feels eerie. A middle-aged man holding a briefcase arrives and I feel a resentful anger towards him for intruding in my world.

Then begins the familiar feel of the wind building, rushing past my face and ruffling my hair as the incoming train pushes the air in front of it and out of the tight tunnel. With a metallic screech of its brakes, the train eventually stops and the doors open right in front of me. A small win.

I was right. Plenty of empty seats, so I take one close to the door, slumping down in preparation for the ride. I pick up a copy of today's free newspaper, discarded on the seat next to me from its previous owner, and begin to flick through it. As the doors begin to beep, warning us that they're about to close, the relative silence is broken by the sound of a child's laugh. It's rare to see children on the tube during rush hour and the sound feels somewhat alien down here.

The laughter, now full-on giggling, comes from a small boy not much younger than William. He's snuggled close to a woman who is obviously his mum. Obvious because it's easy to see the bond of love between them that only a mother and her child can have. She doesn't look like Becky and he doesn't really look like William, but nevertheless, I draw the comparison and I find a smile involuntarily form on my lips.

She's saying something to him which he is obviously finding funny and when she puffs out her cheeks in mock anger, gesticulating wildly and comedically with her hands, I notice the absence of a wedding ring on her finger. Single mum? Divorced? Did she leave him or did he leave her? I suspect he'll have left her, no doubt for a younger version. The world can be a shit place for some people. My stomach sinks sympathetically and whilst the irony of my situation isn't lost on me, I can't help hating this absent man for what he's done to this woman and his son.

I drop my head, feeling for the first time a strong sense of disappointment at myself. This could so easily be Becky and William. Left alone to fend for themselves. Vulnerable, yet their bond growing each day as their little team of two overcomes more and more of the difficulties life throws at them. Clearing each hurdle because, quite simply, they have each other.

I picture their house in the night, the boy fast asleep upstairs and his mum downstairs, sitting on her sofa, alone. The empty void of the space next to her violently loud in the silence. I make a tear slowly trickle down her cheek. Her heart is still a long way from mended.

I'm shaken from my thoughts when the train decelerates quickly as it arrives in the next station. I become aware of the horrible sensation of the lump in my throat and tightness in my chest. My eyes are brimming with unshed tears and the simple realisation that I am close to crying actually makes me cry.

I stand to leave and when I step off the train, I can't help but turn to try and keep watching them for as long as possible. Their happiness is hurting me, but I want it to. I deserve this. Completely engrossed in each other, surrounded by the grimy dirt and harsh mechanical noises, they are a beautiful oasis. It's such an exquisite scene yet my eyes see it with such sadness… and guilt.

The train begins to move away and I watch them leave, following them until the tunnel swallows them up and the last of the carriages noisily vanishes into the gloom.

29

Monday 8:45
Hey you, hope the flight was ok? Thinking of you :)

Tuesday 12:54
Hi. Nice to see the family? Missing you. :(

Wednesday 6:09
Be good to know that you're safe. Please let me know. Wish you were back here.

Wednesday 14:22
Yasmine, it really isn't too much to ask for you to reply to me please.

Wednesday 23:21
I can't believe how selfish you're being!! You throw it on me that you're leaving at the last minute, and then don't even bother to try and get in touch at all. Nothing!

Thursday 3:45
Sorry for last message. Just feeling ignored by you. I imagine you're busy with family etc. Thinking of you a lot. Hope all ok?

A week later and I haven't heard anything from Yasmine. I've played out lots of reasons as to why and I can't get it out of my head that she's with another man there. We've not exactly said we're a couple, Christ, how could I? But she knows we're serious. She knows that. Obviously, we don't see each other that much and there are still so many things I don't know about her and her about me. But we're serious. She should realise that I'm her boyfriend by now, and that there are certain expectations that come with that. Like replying to my texts. Like giving me more notice before leaving the bloody country. Like not fucking other men.

I've been secretly checking my phone every few minutes throughout the day, and at night, when I wake, I take my phone to the bathroom, dimming the screen so as not to wake Becky. I try not to think about what Yasmine was probably doing at that very moment because it's undoubtedly not going to be good.

Amongst all of this mental torture though, I did manage to remember our wedding anniversary. The internet told me that tin or aluminium is the traditional gift for a ten-year anniversary. Given everything that has, and is going on, I didn't think it would be a good option to buy Becky a new set of pots and pans.

Walking back from work one evening in the week, I found myself looking in the window of a jewellers, and before I knew what I was really doing, I'd spent a lot of money on some diamond earrings. I was thinking of Yasmine and how much they would suit her, which made the jolt of satisfaction I felt even more enjoyable, knowing that she wasn't the one to be receiving them. Not after everything she's doing to me.

That was Wednesday afternoon. Today is Saturday, and I'm wandering the aisles of the supermarket looking for inspiration for what I can cook for dinner tonight. We decided, well, Becky decided, that we couldn't leave William with a babysitter, so we will have a special dinner at home when he's gone to bed. Special, in as much as I'll be preparing it.

While Becky is at the hairdressers, I'm to get what I need to cook, and choose a couple of bottles of wine. Afterwards, I'm to take William to McDonalds for a treat dinner as he obviously won't be eating with us. Three quarters of an hour later and I've picked up a tenderloin of pork, looked on the internet for how to cook it, bought the suggested rosemary, mushrooms, spinach, potatoes and jar of applesauce, and collected two bottles of Becky's favourite chardonnay.

Heading to the check-outs, we walk past a display of the latest Spiderman movie. I watch William as he gawps open-mouthed at the cardboard cut-out of the web slinger and the piles of shiny Blu Ray boxes he's peddling.

Sucked in by the colourful marketing, he picks one up and asks, "Can we get one please, Daddy?"

I glance quickly at the front of the box and see the 12A rating.

"William, this is a bit too old for you, mate. Sorry."

"But Daddy," he whines, drawing out the final syllable, "I promise to be good."

"It's not about being good, William. There are things in the film that might scare you. You don't want to have nightmares, do you?"

"But Daddy, I promise I won't be scared," his voice gratingly shrill now.

"William, please! No!" I snap, with a tone that was maybe a bit too harsh in the circumstances. "It's too old for you. It'll scare you, and you probably won't understand what's going on anyway. They put these age ratings on for a reason."

"But Da…"

"William, enough!" I bark and walk away towards the checkouts.

He catches up a few seconds later, and I can see he is trying to fight back tears as he walks a few safe steps behind me.

30

As we walk down the small high street, I try my best to make amends for having to shout at William by offering him a choice for his dinner. When I mention pizza as a potential option, his allegiances towards McDonalds rapidly change, and so we head to the local pizza takeaway instead. I order his pizza and we sit down to wait for it to be cooked. He's unusually quiet still, and I'm sure he's mulling over the incident in the supermarket.

"How come you ordered pepperoni? I thought your favourite pizza was ham and pineapple?"

"It used to be," he replies quietly, but tersely.

"Oh, and what changed then, grumpy guts?" I say, poking him softly in the ticklish part of his ribs, which never fails to make him laugh. Until today.

"I had pepperoni with mum and I liked it better," again, curtly.

It's not usual for him to hold on to bad feelings like this. I plough on.

"So, what do you want to do tomorrow? Fancy taking the football to the park again?"

"Yeah, if you want."

Jesus, he's really making me suffer here. He gets that from his mum.

"Well, I'd like to mate, but only if you want to. Otherwise, we can maybe see if there is something good on at the cinema, or take the bikes to the forest?"

He thinks for a while, and I can see by the curl of the right side of his mouth that he's beginning to break.

"Can we do all of them?"

I laugh. "Well, we can certainly try," I say, hiding my relief, putting an arm around his waist and pulling him in to me for a reconciliatory hug. It's then that I feel something under his jumper.

"What's that?" I ask, squeezing it.

"Nothing."

He wriggles from me, doing his best to hide a concerned look, but failing miserably.

"Well, it's something. What is it, William?"

He keeps quiet, so I put my hand under his jumper, and to my utter disbelief, I pull out a Spiderman DVD case. We both stare at it, and for a few seconds, I can't think of anything to say.

"William!" I say finally, under my breath, trying to avoid a scene. "What have you done?"

He puts his hands between his knees, squeezes them together and his shoulders sag. He looks at the floor, at the space between his fidgeting feet.

"William, I can't believe you've taken this!" The shock starts to hit me more. "You've stolen this. Do you realise that? You've stolen it."

A tear drops onto his scuffed trainer. I can see he's remorseful already, no need to get any more angry, and righteous.

"What made you do that, William?" I ask quietly.

Continuing to look at the floor, he replies meekly, fighting back the tears, "I thought I'd get away with it."

31

"I can't believe he did that," Becky says with astonished disappointment. "What do you think made him do it?"

"I don't know. All kids shoplift once or twice, I know I did. Sweets, though, nothing as expensive as a DVD."

"Some kids might! I didn't and I just didn't expect William to even think about it. Is it something we're doing wrong, Ollie?"

I really wish I hadn't told her, at least not during dinner. I should have kept it until tomorrow. We were having a nice time, but now it seems like the mood has vanished. What else could I have said when she mentioned that she felt William had been quiet all afternoon?

"Honestly, I wouldn't worry about it. It's normal. He was very upset when I told him what he did was wrong. I think he's been scared shitless all day thinking the police were coming for him."

"You should have made him take it back to the shop. He'd have really learnt his lesson then."

"Becky, he was upset enough. He made me promise not to tell you. He's embarrassed. Don't mention anything to him. It won't happen again."

"How do you know?" she says, leaning forward. "I didn't tell you this because you, well, you've been distracted, but he's been getting into trouble at school these last few weeks."

"What happened?"

"His teacher took me to one side when I went to pick up from class last Friday. She said she caught him hitting another boy over the head with wooden bricks."

I smirk, but quickly retreat to a neutral expression because of Becky's terse look.

"It's not funny, Ollie. He made him bleed. Mrs Thomas said she was able to persuade the boy's parents to let it go, but apparently, they were really pissed off. I don't blame them. I was so embarrassed, Ollie."

"Did he say what happened for him to do that? I can't imagine he'd do something like that without a reason."

"He didn't say. He just clammed up. Mrs Thomas said she didn't see or hear anything build up to it. She said she heard a scream, turned around and saw William hitting this boy's head over and over. She said he wouldn't stop until she physically pulled him away."

Shit.

I don't know what to say.

"Shit."

"I can only think he's reacting to what's been happening at home. We've been arguing a bit too much in front of him. Maybe that's making him worry, and he doesn't know how to deal with it. I worry so much about you, Ollie, that I sometimes forget he's there. Perhaps I've said things he shouldn't be hearing."

Shit.

"Listen, you know William," I say calmly. "He was probably provoked by this kid. I'm not saying what he did was right, but I'm sure the little sod deserved it."

"I don't know, Ollie, and that's not the point either. We've not brought him up to use violence."

The sentence hangs in the air, and I take the opportunity to put the chunk of meat into my mouth that has been on my fork, suspended inches from my mouth since she told me about his, what would you call it? Altercation?

"Well, let's keep an eye on it. If he does something naughty again, we'll sit him down and talk it through with him. Sort of three-strikes-and-you're-out. OK?" I say, reaching my hand across the table to hold hers. She shakes her head silently, bereft, as if still unbelieving that her perfect little boy is capable of such things.

"Now, fancy watching Spiderman?"

32

As the train navigates high above the streets of London ready to cross the river, I am resting the side of my head against the train's window, my breath momentarily steaming up the glass, before it quickly clears. I look down to street-level to see the swarms of people rushing to wherever their boxes are for the day. It's an unseasonably cold, grey day and all heads are down, bracing from the chilly wind. Shoulders are stooped and warming arms are wrapped tightly around their bodies or buried deep into pockets.

The train slows to a stop and the driver quickly announces that we are being kept at a light, waiting for our turn to enter the station ahead. From my vantage point, I have a birds-eye view and can intrude on people with impunity. I watch a man in a grey, liveried sweater remonstrate with a traffic warden, throwing his arms towards a parked van next to him. Even though the van is clearly parked illegally on double yellow lines, causing a tailback of traffic behind, I already hate the traffic warden and the authority he represents. I close one eye and place my finger in front of me, which hides the warden completely and makes it look as if the driver is arguing with it. I flick the driver in the head and imagine him flying backwards across the pavement.

In the sea of monochrome, my eye is caught by a woman walking away from me. She is wearing a bright blue wool coat, matching heels, and her long dark hair falls far down her back. She walks beautifully slowly, giving her a sense of being a beacon of calm in the bubbling mess around her. She takes a left turn and disappears behind a building, and for some reason, I feel a sort of emptiness that this woman appeared so briefly in my life before vanishing. I imagine the lines of our lives progressing on a large white background, and hers and mine touching each other momentarily, before diverging away, never to touch again. That was our one moment together, and she didn't have a clue.

Yasmine. It's been thirteen days since our lines went their separate ways, and I'm beginning to think I need to see it for what it is. Did she even go to Canada, or was this just her way of getting rid of me? I keep thinking about my pathetic face when she told me she was leaving, and I'm angry with myself for appearing so weak in front of her. Actually, fuck appearing weak... I *was* weak. Pitiful. Feeble. If she was testing me to see how I coped with her absence, then I've failed with flying colours. Why won't she reply to my messages? Maybe I should call her.

The train jolts forward, my gaze still fixed at the empty corner that blue-coat vanished behind, and rain drops begin to spatter on the misted window in front of me.

33

Not that I ever thought it would, but work does nothing to improve my misery and self-loathing. I know it'll be easier to forget about all of the shit with Yasmine if I keep myself busy. You hear that people 'throw themselves into their work' when they are going through tough times. Well, not this person. I couldn't give two shades of shit about anything or anyone in this place. Actually, that's not true. Keira. I remind myself that I've actually only spoken to this woman once in my life, and I don't really want to think about why I hang so much importance onto her.

Since that first day, I haven't seen her at all around the office, yet I've looked out for her each and every day. My disappointment not fading or waning in any way. If it wasn't for the personal paraphernalia left on her desk, I'd have been convinced that she was just a figment of my imagination.

The fake sunflower sitting in an empty glass. Her brightly coloured mug sat atop a tea-stained coaster. A portrait photograph of a pigtailed girl, her freckled face alight with a gappy smile, school tie awkwardly twisted. A niece perhaps, or goddaughter maybe? There is a warmness I feel from seeing these things, as if they give me more of a glimpse into Keira's life and the person that she is. Sad to say, but I think the plastic sunflower has more of a positive effect on me than any person here.

This morning, as I walk past her desk heading to the office kitchen, there is something incongruous, yet magnificently and obviously different about her desk. Everything is exactly as it has been for weeks, untouched and unmoved, apart from the mug. It's gone, and that simple difference fills me with a nervous excitement. She's here!

What the hell is wrong with me?

I quicken my step and lo and behold, yes! There she is! Her back to me, pouring milk into a bowl of cereal. I used to think that anyone eating their breakfast at work was, well, a bit of a twat to be honest. Fair enough if it's a bacon sandwich or a croissant or something equally portable, but an actual bowl of cereal. That's proper breakfast. Not portable at all. Eating cereal out of a bowl that isn't your own seems somehow wrong. It's impersonal. It's just not normal. I used to think all of that, right up until this very second. Now it just seems quirky and fun.

"Well, hello, stranger," I say casually, trying to hide my elation of her actually being here, right in front of me.

She turns and I'm immediately struck by her sparkling eyes.

"Hello, you!" she says with a mouthful of cereal. Just adorable.

She doesn't quite look how I remember her, which feels strange at first, but I still like what I see. I notice she looks more like pigtails than I realised. Niece then, probably. I want to continue where we left off, so I make my tone playful and flirtatious.

"Long time no see." Play it cool, Oliver. "I thought you might have resigned or something."

She laughs, "I wish! Got bills to pay though before I can plan my escape. How have you been?"

"Oh, you know, same shit, different day. Nothing special has happened around here whilst you've been away," I lie. It doesn't escape my notice that she hasn't told me where she has been.

"Have you been on holiday or something?"

"Well, yes, sort of, I guess. Honeymoon, actually, and let me tell you, coming back here after three weeks in Corsica is particularly difficult to stomach."

A knife twists in my heart.

"Honeymoon? Congratulations!" I think that sounded sincere. "I didn't even know you were engaged." Just saying the words makes me feel sick to my stomach.

"Yes, well I am. Well, was, I guess."

She smiles as if nothing has happened. As if she hasn't led me on. As if she didn't owe it to me to tell me she was engaged. Lying bitch. I want to turn around and walk away, but I swallow down my fury on the hunt for details.

"So…" sound friendly, sound friendly, "…what's his name?"

Why do I even care? Cheating whore. Why do all the women in my life treat me like shit? I resolve that it stops now. Right now.

Her eyes narrow and a wry smirk appears. I notice the crow's feet wrinkles at the corner of her eyes. She looks older somehow. Her skin isn't as radiant as it was, her hair lacks shine. Is that a spot on her chin?

"Actually, her name is Madeline." Well, bugger me. "She's French, hence Corsica. Her uncle let us use his house in Calvi, a little place in the north of the island. It's so beautiful there, have you been?"

I blink a few times, letting this all sink in and I think I shake my head in the meantime.

"Oh, you should go. It's so lovely. Loads of hiking in the mountains, great beaches. The weather is perfect at this time of year."

"Maybe I will. Funnily enough, my wife and I were looking

at holidays last night to celebrate our tenth wedding anniversary. We didn't even consider Corsica."

Yes, my wife of ten years. Piss on you, you duplicitous shit bag.

"She'd love it," she says, unfazed by my mention of Becky.

"I'm not sure, we like to go a bit further away than the Mediterranean. We're not really that sort, if you know what I mean."

She says nothing.

"Well, anyway, glad you had a nice time, but I'd better get back," I say nodding my head towards the office before turning away. "Congrats again."

"Oliver?" Her voice stops me in my place, just inside the doorway.

"Yes?" I say as casually as I can possibly make it sound. It bloody well worked, mentioning Becky. This is where she tells me she's made a terrible mistake, and she hasn't been able to stop thinking about me all through her… honeymoon. Here we go.

"Didn't you come here to get a coffee?" she says, looking at the machine next to her with a look of genial bafflement on her face.

Lost for words, but feeling pretty fucking stupid, I step towards the machine, press the button and stand there, dejectedly, watching the brown liquid take an age to drain into the plastic cup below. From the corner of my eye, I can see she is looking at me, but I don't let on.

Fuck me, does it normally take this long to make a drink?

34

The only benefit of having such a shit day was that it made my decision to go to the bar after work a hell of a lot easier. I decided during the afternoon, and once I'd set my mind to it, the clock seemed to slow down even more. I am under no illusion that I will see Yasmine there, but for some reason, I want to go back to where it all began.

As I walk through the doors, I see the place is fairly quiet. A few tables have been taken up, but I suppose that the cold weather has most people heading straight to the comfort of their own centrally heated homes, with their TV and baggy tracksuits. Most people, but not all.

I make my way towards the bar, order a beer, and take my seat on a bar stool at the lonely end of the long bar. As I wait for my drink to appear, seemingly random thoughts crash in and out of my mind. Spiderman walking through London holding hands with a woman in a blue coat. Kiera's face as she orgasms. Brown rainwater pouring through a dirty street gutter. The bouncer with his face bloodied and beyond recognition as anything remotely human. The beer arrives.

I take a long drink and the harsh bubbles burn the back of my throat, and I relish the sting. I'm startled by a voice right next to me, making me choke on my beer.

"You look like ya needed that."

I turn and look towards the voice.

"Sorry," I cough, trying to clear the tickle from my throat, "do I know you?"

"No, but I know you," he says, the harsh Cockney accent giving his cryptic answer a slightly threatening undertone. "I've seen you about these streets."

The look in his eyes borders on the slightly manic and I sigh inwardly. I come for a quiet drink, or for some other reason, the loonies turn up.

"Really? Like where?"

"E'rywhere mate, e'rywhere!" he laughs loudly.

I should have gone home.

"Right," I say dismissively, turning back to face the bar, hoping he'd get the message.

"You're a mate o' Jay's, int ya?"

I look back at him, studying his pock-marked face for any sign of recognition, but there is absolutely none. His greasy skin shines with a sickly look, and I can see the tip of a faded tattoo creeping up his neck. There is undoubtedly a malevolent edge to him.

"Yeaaa, you is, int ya? I can tell. You're a mate of that smart arse nonce."

"Not really, I met him once a while back. In here, actually. In fact, he was sitting right where you are now, come to think of it, but I wouldn't call him a mate at all. Far from it."

Why am I telling him this?

"I reme'ber," he sneers. "Then that bit a' posh skirt come in. I reme'ber. Tell Vinnie, tell me, tell Vin," he leans in to whisper, and as he speaks, I feel speckles of spit spray across my cheek. "You fucked her, din't ya? You went balls deep in her, din't ya?" He shouts the last sentence and slaps the bar in front of him. I turn to look at the other people here, but thankfully no one appears to have heard.

"Listen, Vinnie, did you say? I don't know you, and to be

honest, I'd prefer just to be on my own if you don't mind."

I stare at him. He leans back, staring intently at me with maniacal eyes, and I can almost hear his thoughts racing through his mind as he considers what to do next. I hold his look, trying to hide my rising unease at the ominous storm brewing. The atmosphere becomes cold.

"Nah, ya don't, mate." His gaze narrows, and he says quietly, "You want me around tonight. You just don't knows it yet."

"No, really, I…."

"Is she comin' 'ere now?" he interrupts. "Is that why you're 'ere? To meet the posh bint?"

"No, she's not. I don't think so anyway. Like I said, I just wanted to be on my…"

"She got rid of ya, din't she? Gave you the ol' elbow hasn't she? What's a'matter?" he says, wiggling his little finger in my face. "You not big enough for 'er?" he sneers.

"Fuck off," I snap, scaring myself because I don't want to goad this idiot into doing something stupid. I look to the bar staff for help, but they're too far away from me, and appear to be paying us no notice at all.

"I can tell ya, ol' Vin would give 'er what she wants, mate." He goes to slap my leg, but seems to think twice and stops his hand just a few inches from my thigh.

"A real good seeing to," he continues. "Listen 'ere," he leans in and says quietly. "I got some good blow for ya… a good fuckin' price as well mate. That'll make it up to ya."

Flash. The feel of Yasmine's tongue on mine as she passes the tablet to me.

With a hesitation that surprises me, I reply meekly, "No. Thanks."

"Yea, you do. You knows you do," he laughs, exposing his

yellowed and broken teeth.

I look down at my open hand and see a small bag of white powder resting upon it. "Smash a bit a this up yer trumpet, get round to her gaff, and give her exactly what she's askin' for." His eyes widen menacingly. "Ya get m' drift?"

"No, really, it's fine." I decide I've had enough and get up to leave before this lunatic does get violent.

"Where the fuck do ya fink you're goin'?" he barks.

"I'm leaving." My tone is much weaker than I'd have liked.

"Go then! Run away, ya bender! You'll never give her what she's deserves!" he shouts after me, as I scurry from the bar. "Vin'll give it to 'er for ya."

35
Two Years Earlier

"Seriously, Cal, you're not driving like this," I say, grasping for the car keys dangling from his hand. "Come on, give me the keys!"

"Don't worry," he slurs, turning from me and walking through the pub's front door. "We'll find a taxi outside."

I swivel my head, aware we have caused a bit of a scene as we've walked through the pub, and the landlord is staring right at me.

"Don't let him drive like that, lad," he warns. "You're in charge, yea?"

I nod my head, "I won't, don't worry."

I walk through the door and I'm immediately hit by the freezing, wintery air. I pull the collar up on my jacket, and, with relief, watch Calum walk past his car, out of the car park and towards the road in search of a taxi. I have to run to catch up with him, and when I do, we walk together to the road in silence.

There isn't a car in sight, which I guess is not surprising at this time of night on a weekday, especially on this quiet country road. It is quickly evident that we didn't have much hope of being able to flag a passing taxi down, yet we stand there for a few minutes, watching the steamy clouds of our breath dance and blow away in the icy breeze.

Eventually, Calum turns to me. "This is hopeless! Come on, I'll drive. I'm not that drunk. I've driven worse."

"Cal, no," I say with force. "Not a chance. You're way over

the limit. Come on, let's go back inside and call for a cab."

I walk back down the pub's long driveway, waiting for Calum to follow. He doesn't immediately, but after a few tense seconds and much to my relief, I hear his feet crunching the gravel below them as he begins walking. The rhythm of his steps speeds up, and before I can work out why, he's jogged straight past me and is heading towards his car, keys jingling in hand.

"Cal, don't you dare!" I shout, but all I hear is his childish giggling.

I run after him, but the effects of the alcohol coupled with the cold slows me enough that he is able to get to his car, unlock the driver's door and jump in. I get to his door just as it slams closed, and I fight with him to open it. "Cal, mate, don't be stupid!" I shout through the window. "Come on out. If we call for a taxi, one will be here really soon."

"We can be home before a taxi turns up." The glass muffles his words, making it sound as if he's underwater. "Anyway, I'm freezing my bollocks off." At which point, he turns the keys in the ignition and the car guns awake.

With a firm, stubborn tone I say, "Well, you can drive yourself if you're going to be a dick. I'm not getting in there with you."

"Suit yourself," he shrugs.

The car's lights turn on, illuminating the car park and the trees in front, and I stand helpless as I watch him reverse out of the car park space. I knew it was a bad idea driving here in the first place, but we were going to miss the start of the quiz, so I'd agreed it was the best plan for us to drive here and taxi back. I should have known this was going to happen.

As he tries to put the car into first, grinding the gears as he does, I bang on the roof, deciding I have to do something to stop him driving.

"Stop. Let me drive at least. I'm not as drunk as you."

His muffled laughter pushes through the window, and he shuffles over the centre console into the passenger seat beside him. As he does, I open the door and get in, all the time knowing what I am doing is completely stupid. But, I hope, not as stupid as watching your best friend drive off into the night as drunk as he is.

I settle into the driver's seat, remind myself of the layout of his car, then hesitate. Calum is obviously aware I am having second thoughts.

"You'll be fine. You've not had that much. And besides, it's fucking cold and we're in the middle of nowhere. We're not going to see any police between here and my place."

He's probably right. I press the clutch down with my left foot, put the car into gear and ease away down the driveway towards the road.

I certainly don't feel drunk, and I console myself that with me driving, we are going to be far safer than if he were driving himself. It is definitely the lesser of two evils, and I don't feel like I have any other option. I check left and right to make sure it's clear, and for good measure, I do it again. Satisfied, I turn left out of the car park and start down the dark country road, the headlights blazing the way ahead for us.

A few minutes pass in total silence. We haven't seen any other cars at all, and thankfully I feel my driving is pretty normal. While I know I'm be over the legal limit, probably twice over, I am feeling OK.

"See," he says, self-righteously. "Fuck all people about. We'll be home before you know it."

"This is stupid," I say. "From now on, we always taxi to this pub. Always."

"Yeah, yeah, we will," he says, laughing as he leans forward to turn the radio on. I immediately turn the volume down, trying to keep unnecessary distractions at bay.

"I reckon we should have gone to speak to those women at the other table. We'd have been in there."

I know he's trying to relax me. Take my mind off of the situation.

"Cal, they were much, much older than us. Some of them looked old enough to be our mums, for God's sake!" I laugh, and I find I'm grateful for the reprieve in the tension I was feeling. "Yeah, but there was one that kept looking at you. She looked a bit younger. She could have taught you a few things, I'm sure. If anything, we could have got a lift home with them," he says, nudging my arm with his elbow.

"You're just wrong, you know that? A deviant."

He laughs.

"Flattery will get you everywhere, my friend."

I can see a tight bend ahead of us where the hedgerows on both sides have been allowed to grow much taller, and as we make our way forward down the narrowing road, I feel claustrophobic and uneasy. I can't see any signs of another car's headlights coming from the other direction, but I still slow down more than I would normally, just to be extra cautious. As we get around the apex of the corner, I can see the road straightens and widens out in front of us, empty of any oncoming traffic.

Just as I think that, a dark mass of something shoots out from the hedgerow to my right, instinctively making me swerve to the left to avoid it. I pump the brakes and the tyres screech on the road in protest, but somehow manage to stick. My heart is pounding with the shock, and Calum's high pitched, panicked scream is ringing in my ears.

"The fuck, Ol!" he screams, half laughing, half gasping. "Woo! That was fucking close!"

"Jesus, my heart's going like the clappers," I pant. "What was that?"

"You're telling me!" he shouts. "I think it was a fox or something."

I breathe out, long and deeply, trying to calm myself from the narrow escape.

"Woo! That was fucking exciting!" Calum shrieks. "I think a little bit of wee came out of me though!" he says with concern, looking down at his crotch. I look too, half expecting to see a wet patch, and that has us both laughing hysterically, the stress dissipating quickly as a result.

Calum reaches out to turn the volume up on the radio, a heavy drum beat of a fast dance song buzzing out of the struggling speakers. I immediately slap away his hand from the volume dial, and in that split second, my eyes are momentarily taken away from the blackness of the road in front of us, and my life changes forever.

It is Calum's scream that shocks me first, my head snapping back up to see the blue Volvo hurtling towards us. I'm immediately conscious I've drifted to the wrong side of the road, and I slam my foot down on the brake pedal as hard as I can, creating an ear-splitting scream from the tyres. Even in that moment, I know that noise will haunt me for the rest of my life. My arms stiffen and my hands grip the steering wheel so tightly that I feel the bones crack within them.

In the last moment before we collide, I look into the car ahead, now just a few feet separating us. The bright beams from my headlights illuminate inside their car, which gives me enough time to register the wide-eyed, horrified faces of a man and woman. Her mouth is open wide in a scream that I can't hear, one of his arms reaching protectively across her chest.

In the initial milliseconds of the explosion of our cars hitting each other, I watch the woman's dark hair whoosh forward over her face as she is propelled forward, and then my own head is smacked violently against the steering wheel.

Everything goes dark.

36
Two Years Earlier, continued...

The first thing I register is the piercing ringing in my ears. It takes all of my energy to open my eyes, and when I do, I have no idea where I am or what has happened. A bright light shines into my face, burning into my retinas and making me wince in agony. I can't hear a thing other than a loud whine in my head. I can barely see. My head is pounding. I lift my head and see a steering wheel in front of me, bent at a strange angle. My consciousness seems to be catching up, and I slowly start to remember where I am and the horror of what just happened. The expression of the woman in the other car is seared into my vision.

I look up and ahead and see the bonnets of our two cars violently meshed together, crumpled in a steaming embrace. Both of the windscreens have gone, forced out by the impact of the collision. My head is swimming. Everything feels dream-like, as if I'm looking at things through someone else's eyes. Only then do I look beyond the crumpled bonnets and into the front of the other car.

The woman is sat, silently staring at me, unable to comprehend what has just happened to her. Her face, lit brightly by a surviving headlight, is deathly pale. A delicate lace of dark, dried blood hangs from her ghostly, white chin. She looks below my gaze, and I follow her. I see the outline of a man, her husband, dying on the bonnet between us. His hand is close enough for me to be able to reach out and hold it. He is completely still, thick blood oozing from his head and matting his hair into a gruesome spike.

Still in shock, I look back at the woman and our eyes lock together over the horror before us. She has a peculiar grimace on her face. A muddle of distress for her husband and malice towards me. She stares at me, and the absolute calm around us amplifies the loud confusion thumping in my head. The silence is broken a few seconds later when she starts to convulse slightly, coughing up a fresh eruption of vivid, red blood from her mouth. I watch her, unable to take my eyes from her, as the life ebbs from her eyes, and her head drops back against her seat.

Numb to any emotion, and unaware of any pain I might be feeling, I notice my mouth feels strange. I explore it with my tongue, and I can feel that a few teeth have been shaken loose by the impact. I wiggle a top molar with my tongue, and the familiar yet peculiar sensation takes me back to being a child again. I feel a thin stream of urine warm my crotch and legs.

Slowly, and still utterly bewildered, I look at the slumped form in the passenger seat next to me. At first, I have no idea who or what it is, and it takes a few seconds for my confused brain to work it out. Calum seems to have come halfway out of his seatbelt, and lies horizontally with his chest across the dashboard, one arm extended out at a peculiar angle in front of him. I reach forward, and grab the back of his jacket and yank him backwards, trying to protect his head from the dangerously sharp remnants of the fractured windscreen. A hot pain sears through my wrist and arm, but I manage to pull him back, his body flopping back into the car, and his head falling into my wet lap.

I look at the side profile of his face. He looks so peaceful and still, as though he is sleeping, and the only thing that suggests he isn't, is the deep, deforming crater in his face. His cheek, eye socket and forehead are sunken and smashed, the skin and muscle unable to hold themselves up without the support of the now shattered skull below it. I stroke his hair, like you would a purring cat, and it is only then that the horrific reality smashes across me. An uncontrollable wail escapes from my mouth, unlike anything I have ever heard before. My own sound, alien to my ears.

I howl and cry as a mix of grief and panic overwhelms me, and I have no idea how much time passes, until eventually, an unbeatable exhaustion consumes me and I pass out.

37
Two Years Earlier, continued...

When I come round, the horror surrounding me snaps me to my senses with a savage brutality. I have survived, when everyone around me hasn't, and a burning need for self-preservation builds within me.

I have no idea how long I've been unconscious for, but the scene in front of me hasn't changed at all. I look around and an unerring clarity of thought spurs me to do exactly what I need to do. I unclip my seat belt and lean against my door to push it open. It's warped and buckled in the twisting of the car's chassis, and so I need to lean my whole body-weight onto it before it starts to move. With a loud, creaking groan, it eventually opens, and I fall heavily and painfully to the cold tarmac below.

I pick myself up and lean back into the car, and with the last bit of energy within me, I grab Calum under his arms and pull him across into the driver's seat. The adrenaline streaming through my veins seems to give me the extra strength I need to move his dead weight across. His left hip, obviously broken, can't control his splayed leg which remains at a vulgar angle, and it takes me a while to pull it up across the gear stick and handbrake, to tuck it under the bent steering wheel. As I grab his left ankle to yank it across, I see the bloodied white tip of splintered bone protruding through the skin of his shin.

I turn to wretch at the gruesomeness, fighting hard to not throw up. When I finally recover myself, I lean back into the car and manhandle his torso into a seated position, pull the seatbelt across him and push it into its clip.

In the darkness, I can make out blue flashing lights drifting from over the distant horizon, out from behind the tall hedgerows, sending a fluorescent, flickering glow into the dark sky above. I realise I'm running out of time, and limp painfully around the back of the car to the passenger side, my right knee refusing to bend and the pain in my head threatening to send me back into unconsciousness. This time, thankfully, the car door opens easily, and I lower myself gently into the passenger seat and click my own seatbelt into place just in time to see the first police car appear from around the corner ahead.

My eyes close.

38

I've been walking for hours in a daze, not sure what to do or where to go. Randomly traversing the maze of London's streets and alleyways. Vinnie's words repeating over and over and over, tormenting my thoughts.

"You'll never give her what she deserves! You'll never give her what she deserves!"

It doesn't seem long ago that I realised I'd unwittingly walked to the train station, but decided to just keep walking past it. It doesn't seem long ago that the crowds had faded away, along with the constant stream of cars and buses. It doesn't seem long ago that the gloom of dusk descended around me, the streetlights came on, and the city became still, and silent, and empty. But when I finally stop walking, miles and miles from where I started, I know exactly where I am.

I look at the building in front of me. The ivory-coloured curtains, drawn closed across both sets of windows, allow a warm, soft light to radiate through them, flickering as the occupant moves around the room. I check my phone. One message from Becky.

Wednesday 19:33

Good work Ollie. You missed his football match. I've just put him to bed. He's been in tears all afternoon because you weren't there. You and I have to have a serious talk. Where the fuck are you?

I picture William crying himself to sleep, wondering why his dad doesn't seem to care about him any more.

I do, William, I do. I'm just… dealing with… things.

While my heart breaks with the pain I'm causing him, the matter that concerns me more right now is that there still isn't a reply from Yasmine. It's still as if she has vanished off the face of the planet.

Except she hasn't. She's here. Behind those ivory curtains.

39

With no hesitation this time, I knock hard on her door, hurting my knuckles as I do. I wait, but I can't hear any movement from inside, so I knock again, harder this time with the meat of my clenched fist. Still nothing, and I feel a desperate anger building within me.

You'll never give her what she deserves.

I bang again, and as I do, the door cracks slowly open until the security chain catches, leaving a tantalising, yet inaccessible glimpse into the hallway behind her. Yasmine's face peers through the crack. She looks miserable, and immediately, I feel the same.

"Can I come in?" I plead.

She looks at me, considering what to do next, and with a deep sigh, she shuts the door. I hear the scratching of the security chain being removed, and eventually, it opens, fully this time, allowing me to step in.

I barely wait until I'm over the threshold before I start.

"What's up? Why didn't you tell me you were back?"

She doesn't answer. Instead, she turns and walks deeper into the house, down the long, tiled corridor and into the kitchen. I follow her.

When I get there, she's already stood facing me, leaning against the solid granite countertop, a large glass of red wine in her hand, and on the counter, a half empty bottle next to a corkscrew with the cork still attached. She is dressed in an oversized t-shirt and baggy tracksuit bottoms that are far too long for her, the extra material ruffling around her bare ankles. Her hair is lank and greasy, looking, like the rest of her, unwashed and dishevelled. Her face, normally so beautiful, is naked with the absence of make-up, exposing the deep lines on her forehead and around her eyes. Her skin, usually so flawless and glowing, is now blotchy and pale. A few angry, red spots surround her mouth. I feel repulsed.

"I've... I've been busy," she replies.

I look her up and down, theatrically presenting my outstretched arms to the untidy room we're in.

"You don't look busy," I say sternly.

The tracksuit, the t-shirt. It dawns on me that they're not hers. They'd fit someone twice her size. A man. But who? A boyfriend? The bouncer? The man from the Christmas photo?

As that thought molests my brain, I look over her shoulder at the fridge and notice that not only has that particular photo been removed, leaving a stark space from its absence, but so has my phone number from her whiteboard. She takes a deep breath, and through pursed lips, she blows out, long and slow, as if gaining resolve.

"Joseph, look, you and me, it needs to stop," she says solemnly.

I feel like I've been punched in the stomach.

Winded.

"I mean, it was fun, but I can't do it any more," she goes on.

Dizzy.

"There's someone else, isn't there?" I say meekly, my voice cracking.

She doesn't answer. Instead, she looks down to her bare feet.

"There is. Was. I don't know. Is... I hope."

"I don't understand." My jaw tightens, and a sickness

overwhelming my stomach, and then it becomes clear to me.

"You didn't even go to Canada, did you?" I bark.

Pause.

"That's not the point. This," she raises her hand towards me, "… this is just wrong."

"Who? Who is it?" I demand.

"It doesn't matter," she says quickly.

"It fucking does to me!" Shouting. "Who?"

"Joe, please!" Pleading. "Don't be like this."

I take a step forward, and she immediately takes a step back in fear.

"Who the fuck is it? Is it him?" I scream, pointing at the missing photograph. "Tell me!"

Her eyes look glassy, as the unshed tears well up.

I close my eyes tight and I see Vinnie's face, his manic eyes staring back at me, his laugh echoing through my skull. You'll never give her what she deserves. I clasp my hands tightly over my ears, trying, but failing, to drown out his cackle. You'll never give her what she deserves. He's fucking her now, but over her moans, I can still hear his vile laugh. *Vin'll give it to her*, he yells, baring his yellow teeth at me. *Vin'll give it to her!* I scream away his words, open my eyes and step towards her.

"You've been fucking someone else behind my back, and you don't even have the fucking decency to tell me who!" I'm in her face now; she has nowhere to retreat to. "I can't fucking believe it you… you fucking ugly whore!"

With that, she slaps me hard across the face. I'm stunned by the strength. Shocked, as the noise echoes around the tiled room. My face stings. I stare at her, her face shocked at her own actions, fear in her eyes. The silence around us becomes muted, my vision darkens around the edges. I hear her say something, but the black water around me muffles her sounds.

Vin'll give it to her.

I grab her throat with one hand, delicate and skinny, squeezing tightly whilst I punch her as hard as I can with my other. I feel the bone and cartilage splinter under my knuckles. Blood spurts from her nose. Her eyes roll back into her skull. I squeeze her throat harder and I feel her larynx crush under my grip. A gurgling noise seeps from her gaping mouth. Her knees give way beneath her and I can't support her weight any more. She drops to the floor. I hear a liquified thud as her head hits the hard granite worktop on its way down, and a second thud as it hits the cold, tiled floor beneath her. Thick, crimson blood oozes slowly out from her splayed hair. I scream at this vision in front of me, but the clarity of the sound breaks the darkness around me. I rise to the water's surface, back into the light of the room.

I look at her and she stares back at me with fear etched across her face. I'm panting heavily. I try to think of something to say to her, but I have nothing. Stunned. Defeated. Sickened. I leave the kitchen and stumble back down the corridor, and as I shut the heavy door behind me, I know I'll never see Yasmine again.

40

I should have called in sick today. After everything that happened yesterday, I have a splitting headache now. I should be at home in bed. But I'm not. I'm at my desk, even earlier than I normally am, because I wanted to leave the house before Becky woke. By the time I got home last night, Becky was already in bed asleep.

I was completely wired. Sitting down, then jumping back up, fidgeting, pacing, mumbling. My mind was racing with bursts of images tormenting me. Traumatising me. Full of intensity and worry, I couldn't turn off. Faces and noises and the voices. The voices obsessively nagging at me. I grabbed at a bottle of whiskey from the cabinet, and began to take large swigs straight from the bottle. Anything to try to stop the voices and numb the electricity crackling within me. At some point, the whiskey must have done the humane thing and knocked me out.

I was grateful to have been able to get in and out of the house without having to face Becky at all. She would be up by now, but she hasn't tried to contact me. For some reason, that pisses me off. Why isn't she concerned about me? For all she knows, I could have been attacked last night and left for dead in some grimy alley somewhere. I should text her and let her know I'm at work. Make up something about a meeting or something. Having to work late last night, and having to come in early this morning to prepare. I won't because I know she won't believe me. I wouldn't either.

At this early hour of the morning, the office is empty, so I take the opportunity to go to the bathroom to try and freshen up a bit. I didn't shower this morning, and the occasional unpleasant bodily smell catches in my nostrils to give away that fact. I look back at my reflection in the mirror. I look as bad as I feel. My eyes are bloodshot, my face pale and damp with sweat, tell-tale dark bags under my eyes. The hair on my face, a few days past what would have been acceptable stubble, now just looks untidy and rough. I notice patches of grey hair around my jawline. That's new. To top the look off, my suit is creased and the white shirt underneath even more so.

I swill cold tap water around my dry mouth, splash my face and try to restyle my unruly hair. You can only put so much glitter on a lump of shit, so I give up and walk out.

Back at my desk, the office is still empty and probably will be for another hour or so. I put my head on my desk and close my eyes for a brief bit of respite.

41

Back in Yasmine's house, the dark night is held at bay by the glow of the lamps and soft candlelight around us. Everything is quiet... peaceful. She holds me tightly against her body, and I can smell her familiar sweet perfume as my face nestles into her warm neck. She runs her hands through my hair and whispers calmly into my ear, "It'll be all right. You'll see." I feel my whole body relax into her, and everything feels better. A bright light comes on to my right, making me instinctively turn to look at it. It's so bright that I can barely open my eyes, and I raise my hand to try to block its harsh glare. Instead of the softness of her neck, I now feel a cruel and cold hardness pressing against my cheek. A familiar thump of a headache returns and I sit up with a startled gasp. The bustling noises of the busy office instantly and violently attack my being.

I rub my eyes and wipe the drool from my mouth. I look around me. No one is paying me any notice at all. I check my watch. 9:45am. Still trying to comprehend that I fell asleep at my desk, I hear Ahmad's voice.

"Morning," he winks. "Rough night?"

I don't say anything, feeling a loneliness at having to lose Yasmine all over again.

"Mate, you look like shit. You should probably go home," he continues.

I think of home, of Becky.

"No, I'm fine. I just had some things to catch up on here. I must have dozed off," I lie. "You should have woken me up."

"I tried," with a breath of a chuckle. "A few times, but you were dead to the world. I decided to let you sleep it off."

Fuck.

"Did Rachel see me?"

A panic rises in me at the thought that the CEO caught me fast asleep at my desk.

"Dunno. She was already in her office by the time I got in."

I feel a crustiness in my eyes and my stomach is uncomfortable. I need to get to the bathroom again to sort myself out. Halfway across the office, I hear a female voice call my name. I ignore it and keep walking, but when I hear it again, this time with a heightened tone of annoyance, I stop.

"Oliver, can I have a word please? In my office."

"I just need to go to the bathr…"

"Now, please."

I can tell by her tone that this is not a stand-off I can win, so I follow Rachel across the floor to her office.

Once there, she instructs me to sit down, which I do, and whilst I fumble to straighten my jacket and pat down my shirt, she is closing the blinds of her fishbowl office to give us some privacy. She walks past me and I get a delicate waft of her perfume as she takes a seat behind her large, mahogany desk.

"Oliver, do you know why I've brought you in here?"

Fuck me, I feel like a naughty schoolboy in the headmistress's office.

"No, not really," I reply sheepishly.

She looks at me, disappointed and minutely shakes her head.

"I brought you in here because we've all noticed a considerable and sustained drop in your efforts. You're barely accomplishing anything during the days, and you're leaving the office earlier and earlier. I've had complaints that you're not turning up for some meetings. You're just not delivering, Oliver."

She stops talking, leaving a long, uncomfortable silence into which I am meant to reply. So I don't.

"Is there anything going on that I should be aware of, Oliver? Anything at home? Anything here?"

"I'm sorry. I know I've not been myself here of late, but things are… I search for the right word, "challenging at home at the moment."

"Oliver, I'm sorry to hear that, I really am. But difficult as it may be, home is home, and work is work. You have to leave all of that at the door when you come in here."

I look at my feet. "You're right. I'm sorry."

"Did you even go home last night? You look terrible."

I'm surprised that her voice seems caring now, but I also notice she is resting a long finger under her nose, as if to try and block out an unpleasant smell.

"You know, if you're struggling, there are places you can go to, people you can talk to. People trained to be able to help alcohol dependent peo…"

"It's not that," I cut her off. "I'm not an alcoholic."

I try to swallow away the growing lump in my throat.

"What is it then, Oliver? We can't have this sort of behaviour continue, can we?"

"No." She's right. "No, you're right. I'll sort it out, I promise."

I hear my words and even I'm not convinced by them. The silence in the room is deafening. Eventually, after what seems like an eternity, Rachel speaks.

"Be sure that you do. Go home now. Take a shower. Try and eat something. Talk to your wife. Sort out whatever is doing this to you." She sounds truly concerned, and the compassion in her voice makes me well up. I feel overwhelmed that someone finally appears to care for me. I wipe a tear from my eye before it can fall and stand to leave.

"Thank you," I say, meekly, my voice breaking.

"But Oliver," more authoritative now. "This is a warning. If we have to have this conversation again, it'll be the last one we have with you working in this company. Are we clear on that?"

I nod a silent agreement.

"Good. Now go home."

42

Of course, I can't go home. I obviously can't go back to work, which is why I find myself aimlessly wandering the streets yet again. Lacking energy, I see a bench up ahead of me, and I walk over to take a seat. My head slumps towards the ground and I watch the expensive polished leather shoes and power heels pass by me. Each shoe on the feet of someone who knows exactly where they're going. In control of themselves and the future. I look at my own dirty shoes, worn and scuffed. Pathetic. I bring the brown paper bag to my lips, and drink from the cheap whiskey bottle within it, feeling a comforting warmth surge across my chest.

No, I'm not an alcoholic, Rachel. But it's only the drink that can hush the noises in my head. It dampens the sound of screeching tyres. It stifles Calum's terrified scream. It deadens the metallic explosion of the cars smashing into each other.

It used to.

43

I find myself in a quiet part of the city, far away from the disapproving frowns and tuts of the judgemental passers-by. Stumbling across pavements and across roads, the fogginess in my head is destroying my coordination and making each step feel heavy and mistake-laden. I can see the steam of my breath, which tells me the weather is cold, but I don't feel it at all. The once vibrant and colourful city that I was starting to enjoy, now just a grey, lonely, incessant shit hole. Just a few weeks ago, I was walking these streets, arm-in-arm with Yasmine, feeling like a king, and now all that was good has been obliterated. All around me, cruel echoes of what once was, compounding what I'm losing.

I catch myself in the reflection of a darkened shop window and I stop to take a longer look. I barely recognise the face that glares back at me. The dark glass painting evil looking shadows across my face. I try to focus my blurred vision, batting away the swirling circles of muted colours of what is behind me. I blink more and squint, attempting to bring the words above my head into focus. Unsteady on my feet, the words slowly begin to materialise from the blur. I can make out some of the reversed letters, but putting them together into words is too much for my fucked-up brain to cope with, so I give up and turn around to see what it says.

'The Crown.'

From the outside, this dingy looking pub looks the antithesis of the plush, expensive bar I met Jay and Vinnie in, and of course,

Yasmine. My heart sinks with the reminder of just how far I've fallen from that day.

I stumble and crash through the door, and immediately I feel more comfortable in my surroundings. There is a smattering of grubby looking men dotted around. Half-drunk pints of beer in hand. Copies of horse racing newspapers and red-topped tabloids lie on the tables in front of them. It's a place of dirty fingernails, unwashed t-shirts and overstretched, stained sweaters emblazoned with various brand names you'd only find in low-end sports shops at the wrong end of the high street. A dusty television set rests on an insufficient looking shelf high up in the corner of the room, its wires untidily spilling out from behind it. I recognise the day-time TV program and for that reason, I'm very glad it's on mute.

There's not a smile to be seen anywhere. Not a conversation to be heard. Nothing. Just a sorry collective of broken souls who have found a level of understanding amongst each other, and escaped the harshly critical city behind the old door I've just come through.

I order a beer and head straight to the toilet to empty my painfully full bladder. When I get back into the bar, my drink is waiting on the bar for me, fizzing and sparkling tantalisingly. I pick it up and head to a table in the bleakest corner of the gloomy room, as far away from everyone else as possible. I need time to think.

I sit down with an appreciative sigh as the weight is taken from my legs. It feels good to bend my knees. I curl my back, trying to stretch the stiffness away. A big, deep breath and a moment of calm respite allows the first clear thought I've had for some time to materialise in my head. Becky. I check my phone and unsurprisingly, there is a message from her.

Thursday 13:12

I've taken William. We're going to stay at my mum's. I can't help you if you won't help yourself. You're killing me, Ollie. You're killing us. Don't get in touch. I need space from you.

She's left me.

Nothing within me registers surprise. I'm aware I'm too drunk to really grasp the magnitude of what has just happened, but I know the impact will eventually catch up with me and have an enormous effect on me. My best friend. My job. My... what would you call her? My mistress? Lover? Girlfriend? And now my wife and son. Anyone important to me, I've destroyed them all. How did this happen? Why can't I stop this?

For the second time today, my throat tightens and my eyes fill with tears. I keep staring at the text message, and a tear escapes, and runs down my cheek, before dripping on to the phone screen in my hand. I drop the phone onto the sticky table in front of me and bury my face into my hands, hoping and wishing that when I take them away again, I'll wake up and find this has all been a terrible nightmare.

Everything inside of me shatters.

"Well, would you look at what the cat dragged in?"

Unbelieving, I take my hands from my face, and look towards the source of the voice. How the fuck has he found me here, of all places?

"Please," I beg. "I just want to be on my own. I'm serious now. Leave me alone."

"Is that the way you greet your friends?" Another voice to my right. I cannot quite fathom what is going on. A deeply unsettling, almost monstrous sensation washes over me. How have they found me? In this random part of the city. Why are they here? Surely this has to be a bad dream. It has to be! This can't be happening to me.

But there is no denying it, Jay and Vinnie sit on either side of me.

"What are you... how the hell did you find me here?" I ask incredulously.

"I guess it's fate," replies Jay, beaming with his perfect smile, his whole refined being looking so out of place in these grim surroundings. "I suppose we were always going to end up here at some point, weren't we?"

"You really do know each other," I mutter, looking at Jay, but pointing over my shoulder back at Vinnie.

"I told ya din't I? Jay and me go way back. We've been around for fuck knows 'ow long, in't we, Jay m'boy?"

"Unfortunately, yes," replies Jay sarcastically and with a derisive smile. "For quite a few years now."

They are such an unlikely pair, that I find it hard to comprehend that these two would ever find themselves in the same sorts of places to meet, never mind to actually talk and become and stay friends. Vinnie, malevolent and sinister. He belongs in the darkness, away from people like Jay. And Jay, well, he belongs in a swanky corner office of a beautiful skyscraper, high up above everyone else, carving out a life full of achievement and happiness.

"We saw you walk by the bar a few hours ago," Jay admits. "You looked a little worse for wear, if I'm honest. You looked like you needed us, so we followed you."

"In fact, we 'ad a bet, din't we Jay?"

"He's right, we did," Jay says matter-of-factly before saying in a mock scolding tone. "But you let me down, Joe. Or should I say Oliver. You're more of an Oliver now. Yes, I said you'd end up in a nice bar, and we'd find you chatting up a beautiful looking lady."

"Fucking nonce!" Vin chimes in. "I said you'd end up in a pub, being a miserable pussy and drowning yer sorrows. And look where you are?" he says triumphantly.

"Yes, but Vincent, listen. He went to that off-license first for a naughty bottle of whiskey, so neither of us were right."

"Fuck off, Jay! We're in a shitty pub now, in't we?" he says angrily. They are just not compatible with each other.

"Well, I can't argue with that, my friend. I can't argue with that," says Jay, chuckling to himself at the unfathomable situation. "So, Oliver, tell us. Why are we all here? Why did I lose the bet today, my friend?"

While this conversation has been going on between them, I stare down at my feet, just visible under the table in front of me. I'm hearing their words, but I'm thinking of Becky and William, and what I've done to bring this terrible situation around.

"She left me," I mumble weakly.

"Hmm, yes, we know. And Yasmine… she's gone too, hasn't she?" Jay says quietly.

I'm stunned that Jay knows her name, but then I guess he must have remembered it from the first night we all met, and obviously Vin has told him about his and my last conversation together. If that's what you'd call it.

I nod my head.

"Sounds like quite a pickle we're in here, Oliver," Jay sighs.

"Quite a fucking Elliot," Vinnie sneers.

Jay looks sideways at his friend with a look of confusion.

"A what? An Elliot?"

"An Elliot… Elliot Ness… mess, you posh prick! Basically, the lads fucked it, ain't he? Right royally fucked it all up!"

I see Jay from the corner of my eye, frowning and shaking

his head slightly in bewilderment at his crass counterpart. These two just do not belong together. It's so illogical.

"Right. Well, yes, it's a mess," he says, turning back to me. "So what are we going to do about it all, Oliver? How can we fix this?"

My head is swimming with the effects of the alcohol, and my vision smears as I shake my head at him.

"I don't know. I just don't know." I look to Jay as the only apparently sensible and sober person here. "Help me, Jay. What should I do?"

"Well, the way I see it, is you've got a few options. One, stand up, go home, sleep this off, and tomorrow morning, when your head is right, call your wife and apologise. Promise you'll fix everything between you. Then go in to work and buck your ideas up there."

"I dunno, Jay. Sounds fucking borin' to me," mutters Vin.

"Or option two, you stay here with us, we'll get some more drinks in, and just forget about it all until another time. Work it out tomorrow."

"Now you're talkin' my language, Jay me ol' mate!"

He's right. Jay that is, not Vinnie. I feel at a crossroads. One way is a long and winding road back to Becky and William and salvation. I actually picture in my head a yellow brick road ahead of me, and the tune tinkles in my head.

Follow the yellow brick road.

As good as the option sounds, I can't make Becky appear there. Try as I might, clouded and foggy, my mind cannot place Becky at the end of this road.

Follow, follow, follow, follow, follow the yellow brick road.

I don't feel as if I've got it in me to take that path yet. I'm not ready.

But the second option? Nothing good can come from it. Nothing at all. But it's easy. I can just sit here and do it. I'm already in place. It's not as if I can do anything worthwhile now anyway, can I? I'm no good for any of it at the moment. Maybe I need to just sit it out and talk this all through with Jay. Maybe it'll help, getting his perspective. Maybe it's for the best.

We're off to see the Wizard. The wonderful Wizard of Oz.

"'Scuse me, mate," I call to the barman. "Three large whiskeys please."

"You fuckin' beauty!" Vin cackles.

44

The pub is louder now. Well, we are louder at least. The rest of the pub is probably the same as it was when I came in hours ago. I notice the occasional pissed off glances from the other drinkers towards my table, but fuck them. Fuck them all. Miserable arseholes.

"What the fuck you looking at, hey?" I jump to my feet and slur at one of the old shit heads. "Fucking prick. Turn around and mind your own fucking business."

Vin cackles his appreciation.

"Yeah, just mind your own fucking business," I murmur under my breath as I sit back down.

"All right there, champ!" Jay pats my shoulders and rubs them, as if I am a fighter in the ring and he is my trainer. "I think you've scared him enough."

"Barman!" I shout, scanning around the room for him. My eyesight takes a few weird seconds to catch up with my head's movement, everything stays blurred and frayed at the edges until it does. "Barman, another round," I stammer, trying to sound jocular and friendly. I still can't find him, and for a moment slump back into my seat in defeat.

I rest my eyes on the TV high up in the corner of the room. I fight to keep my heavy eyelids from shutting, and I squint to focus on the screen. There is a man sitting behind a table adorned with various microphones and a senior looking policeman next to him. They both look pretty fucking miserable. Something shit must have happened. Though it might just be a TV crime drama,

I just can't tell.

I hiccup and the force of it makes my eyes slowly close. I'm overwhelmed by how unbelievably tired I feel now. My neck and head are becoming too heavy to hold up. Another hiccup and I momentarily stir awake. I lift my head, force my eyes to open, but only the one of them acquiesces. The man on the TV wipes a tear from his eye with the back of his hand, and a myriad of camera flashes light up his face, each one trying to capture the poor sod at his most miserable point.

"Fucking press," I belch. "They're like fucking vultures. Look, look, Jay. Look. They're just trying to cash in on someone's misery."

My other eyelid finally unsticks itself, and after a few blinks to try to focus my vision, I realise I recognise the man from somewhere, but I can't picture where. He's probably some twat celebrity caught kiddy-fiddling or something, and now he's been caught, he's all apologetic. Pathetic. In that case, keep taking the pictures of the pervert!

I still think it might just be a TV drama though.

Another hiccup brings an acidic bile up into my throat, which I try to wash down with the last remnants of the dark, flat beer in front of me.

"Fuck her," I say to no one in particular. "Fuck her and her fucking judgements. She's not exactly Mrs-fucking-perfect either."

I'm thinking about Becky and Matt on Facebook, and the memory of the photo smacks me hard across the face. His scummy hand on her hip. Hang on a minute! It just occurred to me that going back to her parents means going back home, to where everything else is, where everybody is. Including Matt.

"Fucking bitch," I mutter inwardly.

"Yeah, fuck 'er," Vinnie says with a snarl. At least he agrees with me.

"I knew I shouldn't have married her. I settled too early. You know what I mean? I could have done better. I should have stayed single, then moved down here. I'd have had my pick of them."

I'm slurring. Stop slurring.

"'Course you would have."

"Jay, I could and you know it. Me and you, out together. Watch out ladies, here we come!"

I jump to my feet, clapping my hands together, knocking the table in front of me with my knees, spilling beer and toppling a few empty pint glasses to the floor, smashing them.

"Oi, you!" A strange bark from the other side of the pub. "I've just about had enough of you! Get out of my pub!"

It's the landlord.

I raise my hands in apology and try to speak without laughing. "Sorry, sorry. We'll be good, I promise. Sorry."

He walks over to me, and as he does, a few of his customers get up and walk behind him.

"But before you go," he says with venom in this voice. "You've run up quite a bill."

I didn't notice how worryingly big he was when I came in. Overweight with it, but I can see strength in his thick arms as he crosses them in front of himself. Careful.

"OK, OK, no problem," I say, taking my wallet from my pocket. "How much do I owe you?"

He grabs the wallet from my hand, opens it and takes the £200 I took out from the cash machine earlier this afternoon.

"This will cover it and the breakages."

"Wait, wait, that's much more than I owe you, surely," I say, struggling to speak the words, my tongue feeling thick in my mouth. "Come on, let's be reasonable here."

He flicks my now empty wallet onto the table in front of me, making sure it lands in the puddle of spilt beer. Prick.

"Get out," he snarls with real menace in his tone, as he pockets my cash.

I sneer at him and wait, expectantly, for the dark water to rush in and begin to drown me, but for some reason it doesn't come. After a few seconds of silence, I smile, shrug.

"OK, you win. Come on, lads, let's get out of this shithole and leave these sorry fuck heads to their miserable fucking existences." I turn to Jay on my right, but he's not there. Slightly panicked, I look to the left for Vinnie, but he's gone too. Arseholes! They must have slipped out quietly when all this started to kick off. Fucking cowards.

Even drunk, I'm fully aware of the precarious situation I have found myself in, so I grab my wallet from the table and walk out quickly, making sure not to look back.

45

I stumble out of the door, and I'm immediately disoriented by the unexpected dark shroud of night that has descended. I check my watch and after struggling to focus, I see it's just short of midnight. After the shit storm inside, my veins feel as if they are burning like a crackling fire. An aggressive energy I've never felt this intensely before effervesces inside my whole body. I have no idea where I am, so I head back the way I think I came earlier today. An invisible and unspent force within me makes me twitch and tremble with every step.

The streets around me are peaceful and empty. The only noise is the clicking of my heels on the stone pavement beneath my feet. The tranquillity amplifies the torrent of whispering voices in my head, and the tick, tick, ticking of my shoes, malevolently mimicking the timer on a bomb. Soon to explode. Unsteady on my feet, I stagger along. Just then, from behind me, an ear-splitting, screeching crash startles and chills me to my core.

"Wha' the fuck were that?"

"Jesus Christ, Vinnie! You scared the living shit out of me! Do that again and I'll fucking kill you, I swear!" I scream, trying to get my gasping breaths under control. I lower my tight fists, instinctively raised to shield my head, remnants of a distant primordial survival reaction.

"Joe, my friend, that was something to behold," laughs Jay. "Really, that was amazing. I didn't know you had it in you!"

"I told ya, din't I, Jay, he's a wrong 'un, mate." Vinnie pushes his face closer to mine, a dark, sinister and deeply unsettling look. He whispers, "You're a fuckin' wrong 'un mate, aren't you? You're touched, geezer. Un-fucking-hinged."

"Leave him, Vincent," Jay demands.

But Vinnie just keeps staring at me, menacingly swaying from side to side, inching his face uncomfortably closer and closer, so that all I can see is his wide-eyed maniacal expression. All I can smell is his stale, putrid breath. His words echo relentlessly through my brain. Every piece of me wants to kill him. To grab his throat with the tips of my fingers, and squeeze and squeeze and squeeze until they break through his slimy, pale skin. Squeeze until I can feel the hard cartilage of his larynx. Squeeze until my fingers slip behind it so that I can grip it all as hard as I can.

Rip his throat out his neck.

Feel the warm, blood-speckled air burst from his trachea and on to my knuckles.

Feel his thick, hot blood coat my hand and pour down my forearm.

Taste the metallic air.

But I don't. Instead, I turn away from him and look down the length of dimly lit street, hemmed in by the valley of darkened buildings on either side of it. In the distance, and for a brief second, I see the side of a double decker bus, its lights illuminating its innards, as it speeds past, vanishing as quickly as it appeared.

Amongst the deafening confusion in my mind, I know I need to go home, and down that street is the way I think I need to walk. I can hear a buzzing sound getting louder in my head.

Home.

Becky.

I pull out my mobile phone, wondering if she's tried to call, but my woolly vision doesn't work well enough for me to focus on it.

The buzzing gets louder.

I squeeze my eyes closed tight, and open them, hoping my eyes will clear. It doesn't. I hold the phone at arm's length, as if distance will help my vision. As the screen starts to become more defined in my view, the buzzing reaches a crescendo, and my hand is hit hard and painfully by something that flies past me, sending my phone crashing to the ground. For whatever reason, I instinctively grab at what has hit me.

An arm. The arm of a rider on a moped, darkly dressed, his face hidden by his black helmet. All of this I see in an instant. The speed at which he hurtles past me means as quickly as I grip onto his arm, it is torn away, lurching me forward and throwing me down to the pavement below.

As I'm falling, I look up and see the driver continue further down the road. I can see he is completely out of control, unbalanced by my attempts to grab him. His bike wobbles one way as his body jerks the other, until eventually he collides heavily with a lamppost at the edge of the pavement. My hands hit the ground, but still, I watch as he flies through the air, his feet circling over his head, until he lands on the road with a sickening thud. His bike crashes down a few feet from him and for a few long seconds, the only movement is the back tyre still spinning. The only sound, the moped's indicator light ticking on and off, on and off.

The whispers have stopped.

Time stands still, and lying face down on the cold floor, I try to make sense of what has just happened. I think he had tried to steal my phone from me as he drove by. I lie in shock for a few seconds, watching the rider lie still by his bike. I slowly, and painfully, begin to pick myself up.

The light from the indicator flashes on, illuminating the scene in an amber haze, and then blinks off, exaggerating the darkness surrounding us all. In between the flashes, I notice the rider's body move slightly.

Off, he's gone.

On, his knee has bent up.

Off, darkness.

On, his arm has reached out above him.

Off.

On, he reaches around his body to try and twist himself off his back.

Off. On. Off. On. Off.

I feel hypnotised, unable to take my eyes off of this intriguing light show.

Then a shrill animalistic screech pierces the silence.

Vinnie runs past me, straight up to the rider, now doubled over, resting on his knees and elbows. The indicator rhythmically lights the scene in front of me, and it appears Vinnie is kicking the man with huge force in the stomach.

Off. On.

The rider collapses to the floor, and gasping for air, rolls on to his back, his hands trying to cover his stomach.

Off. On.

Another kick, even harder this time, into the exposed ribs.

Off. On.

Again, in the same place, this time I hear a sickening cracking sound as the ribs give way under the pointed shoes. A fourth kick, more crunching and snapping of bones. All I can hear is Vinnie's snorting and the muffled, gasping screams emanating from within the rider's helmet.

Barely moving now, the driver starts to fumble inside of his jacket, taking advantage of the momentarily gap that Vinnie takes to get his breath back. At first, I think he's trying to feel and protect his injuries, until his hand comes out from under his jacket and I see. A quivering hand holds weakly on to a long-bladed knife. I can see, probably from the injuries of the crash and subsequent attack that he is struggling to grip it properly, and Vinnie quickly kicks it away from him.

The knife slides and comes to a stop close to me, and though I intuitively bend down, it is Vinnie who picks it up. He grasps the wooden handle and turns the knife slowly, inspecting it from every angle. The amber indicator light flickering on and off gives the blade a menacing glint.

Vinnie looks down at the rider, who is still writhing in agony on the floor, gasping for breath, and unable to get to his feet. He looks back to the knife. I can tell exactly what is going through his demented head and I try to scream for him to stop and put the knife down, but when I open my mouth, nothing comes out.

I watch everything unfold in front of my eyes, feeling like I'm caught in a nightmare that I desperately want to wake up from. Vinnie drops to his knees and slowly manoeuvres the knife in his hand, so that he can grip it tightly with the blade now protruding from the underside of his clenched fist. He raises his hand high above his head, the blade glinting with violence in the flashing orange light. I can't stop him.

"No, don't!" Jay howls, the desperation in his voice penetrating my skull, but it has no effect on Vinnie who seems not to hear him. Instead, he pounds his fist down hard and fast onto the rider's chest with a strange, muted thud. The world seems to stop revolving, nothing else could possibly be happening other than this terror unfolding in front of my eyes.

I watch in horror as the tip of the knife pierces the rider's t-shirt. I feel as if I can hear each strand of cotton break and snap as the sharp blade slices through. I am the knife. As though in slow motion, I visualise that I am the tip of the blade, and I continue deep into the chest of the rider. I can see everything inside of him. I see the knife slicing through the thin chest muscle, deflecting past the protective bone of the sternum, and through, far down into the heart's ventricle, nicking the pulmonary artery, before bringing my murderous plunge to a rest in the upper lobe of the lung.

"Stop! Stop!" Jay's screams echo around me.

As the blade begins its brutal journey back the way it came, the gap behind everything it has mortally wounded is quickly filled with oxygen pouring out of the stabbed lung, mixing with the thick arterial blood and creating a squelching, frothing red explosion.

Jay shrieks in panic, "No!"

The blade now fully removed from the chest, blood pulses and spits angrily from the wound, spattering Vinnie's face and arms, flicking into his open mouth as he screams a bestial roar. The knife is back high over his shoulder. Suddenly, time races back to normal speed, just as he plunges it back down. The rider holds his hands in front of him in a futile attempt to protect himself from the repeat blow. This time the knife cuts easily though the fingers of one hand, slicing the middle finger so that it is only held on by a few sinews of intact muscle. The power of the strike pushes the hungry blade through the hand and back into the dying man's chest.

Again, the knife rises, glinting in the amber light, before cutting back into the man's body. Again, and again, and again.

The blood splatters and sprays with each frenzied hit. The rider has long since stopped moving, and his blood stains under him in a dark, glossy pool. But the hits keep on raining down across his stomach, chest, shoulders, neck and arms.

Vinnie raises his blood-slicked hand over his head for yet another hit, but mercifully the blade has gone, snapped and held deep in a vertebra of the rider's spinal column. He only realises when he hits down on the pulped-up chest, and the sensation is different. There is no longer the feeling of slicing through flesh, replaced by a dull thud of a punch. Confused, he looks in horror at the wooden handle in his hand as though he has no idea what it is, before throwing it to the side, as if finally frightened back to sanity from what he has done.

He stands, and I'm struck by how quiet everything has become, the silence gushing in to fill the void left by the frenzied screaming, brutal sounds of terror and ripping flesh. I look down at myself and see my jacket is heavily stained with this man's blood. I run as fast as my legs can take me, fuelled by a tidal wave of uncontrollable panic. I run through the dark side streets, putting as much distance between myself and the ferocious murder that has just happened.

I keep running until I can't breathe any more. My lungs are burning and I can't seem to get enough oxygen into them. The searing pain across my whole protesting body is too much to cope with. I stop running and immediately vomit the contents of my stomach onto the road and wall of the alleyway I am in, splashing my trousers and shoes with a gelatinous, brown liquid. Even though there is nothing left in me to bring up, I can't stop the violent heaving and retching which makes my stomach hurt even more. Tears stream from my face and I start to sob quietly, somehow, in all of the madness, aware that I need to remain unseen. After a short while, I know I must keep moving. I fight to control my tears and wipe my sticky mouth with the sleeve of my shirt, before leaving, not just the dark alleyway behind me, but also the terror.

46

The warming sunshine pours into the bedroom and slowly wakes me from a fitful sleep. I keep my eyes closed and take a deep, contented breath. The bright sunlight is transformed in colour by my eyelids. From white, to a relaxing red. Focus on something. Feel the soft bed sheets under me, and the toasty, cocooning quilt gently hugging me. Another deep breath in.

When I do eventually open my eyes, the cheerful rays welcome me to the day, warming my face and creating a feel-good vibrancy within me. I would normally have drawn the curtains before going to bed, but lying here now, watching the wispy clouds tumble across the azure blue sky, I'm glad I forgot.

I turn my head to the empty space where Becky usually lies but I don't feel sadness, only positivity. I'm sure that today is going to be a great day, that I will talk to her later, and soon after, she and William will be home. I look at the clock. I'm going to be late for work, but I don't mind.

I swing my legs out from under the quilt and enjoy the sensation of the soft, thick carpet under my feet. There is a familiarity in the texture of it, and watching my toes scrunch up, I realise it's almost exactly the same as the carpet from my boyhood bedroom back at Mum's. I don't think I've ever noticed it before, but it evokes a wonderfully soothing sensation in my heart. I stretch out the sleep-induced tightness in my back and shoulders, rotate my head to hear the satisfying cracks of the stiff muscles and bones loudly in my skull, stand up and head into the bathroom.

The sensation of the hot shower on my face feels amazingly invigorating. I leave the supermarket-own-brand shower gel and decide to treat myself to using the expensive soap that Becky bought me for last Father's Day. The soft lather spreads luxuriously across my chest and arms, and the rich smell of sandalwood and spices infusing with the steamy shower further relaxes me. I notice that the underneath of my fingernails are unusually dirty, so I use Becky's wooden nail brush to get rid of whatever it is, until the edges of the nails are clear and white again. Even though I finished rinsing a while ago, I find myself paralysed from the comfort of the shower, unable to step out as the hot jets of water needle into my shoulders and back. I look down and watch the water run down the outside of my arm, and pour from the tip of my little finger. I move my hand, aiming so that the stream of water hits my feet. I'm trapped by luxury.

When I do eventually turn the shower off, I let the last drops of water fall from me, pull back the shower curtain and reach for my towel. When I wrap it around me, I feel its cold dampness. I must have used it last night, but I don't recall having a shower when I got home. I don't really remember getting home, but I know I was drinking, so maybe that isn't a surprise. Still, I wrap it around me and close my eyes, imagining the usual sounds of the house in the morning. William's heavy stomping as he runs across the upstairs floor getting ready for school. From the kitchen, the distant radio show plays the nineties songs that Becky loves to listen to, while she prepares William's breakfast and lunchbox. I know that today is going to be a great day.

Back in the bedroom, I pick out a crisp white shirt, and, assuming that the sunshine is already heating up the day, I decide not to bother putting a suit on, opting instead for a pair of dark blue chinos instead.

I pick up my mobile phone from the bedside table, noticing that one, my battery is low, and two, I haven't had any messages from Becky. No problem on both counts. I have a charger in my desk at work, and I will write to Becky now. I open up my messages and reread what she sent me last.

Thursday 13:12
I've taken William. We're going to stay at my mum's. I can't help you if you won't help yourself. You're killing me, Ollie. You're killing us. Don't get in touch. I need space from you.

There is nothing I can't fix when I'm feeling like this. I type my reply.

Friday 8:45
Becky, I'm sorry I made you go to such extremes, but please know that I love you and William very much, and I will do anything you want to get you both back.
I love you x

I don't expect her to reply any time soon, given what she said, but I'm willing to play the long game with her. I just want them back in my life, now that everything finally feels better.

I walk down the stairs and into the kitchen. I'm singing the verse to a terrible girl band song that I know Becky liked when she was a teenager. I know I'm getting all the lyrics completely wrong, but the general tune is there, and somehow it helps bring her back to this room.

I'm starving, and I open the cupboard where the breakfast stuff usually is. I squeeze the plastic bag holding a solitary croissant, but it feels hard and stale so I leave it where it is. I pick up the box of bran flakes and give it a shake. Almost empty.

Behind it, a bright yellow box adorned with Coco the Monkey smiling inanely at me, which for some reason resonates uncomfortably with me. I must be missing William more than I thought.

I decide that I'll grab some breakfast on the walk in to the office. I step out of the front door, and I'm hit by the morning's comforting warmth, so I roll up my sleeves for the walk to the station. I check my phone and I see the glorious word under my text to Becky.

Read.

I picture her reading the message and her smile lighting up her face. Her beautiful smile.

47

There are lots of benefits to getting a late train into the city, but the most obvious is the fact that the trains are largely empty, and so I have my pick of the seats. I decide on one by the window and, not wanting to drain the precious last few squirts of battery power in case Becky calls, I don't bother putting any music on. Anyway, there is no need to block the world out today.

I opt to sit on the sunny side of the train so that I can enjoy the bright warmth on my face. As the train makes its way along the tracks, I'm amazed by how green and vibrant everything is outside. As if a cloak of grey has been lifted from the world and the vivid colours of the trees have come out to dance. I can't help but feel hugely optimistic.

The train soon pulls to a stop in the next station and I watch a large grey squirrel chase another around a tall oak tree behind the station house. The tree is almost luminous in the brightness, and the way the branches and leaves move from the squirrels makes me think of that scene from Jurassic Park. I can't wait until William is old enough to watch that. He'll love it.

The one much smaller squirrel being chased gets to the end of a long branch, and with nowhere left to escape, chooses to try his luck and jump across the huge void to the neighbouring silver birch tree. At first, the gap seems far too wide, but to give him credit and perhaps owing to the fact that he has no other option, he gives it a go. He majestically sails through the air and just about makes it, although I'm not really sure how. The pursuing bully squirrel, getting to the end of the same branch, assesses the situation and decides the jump is too much for him and his bulk. He turns dejectedly and scampers back up the branch, and I lose sight of him behind the thick foliage. I look back at the smaller squirrel and he's grooming his tail with his paws, apparently already recovered from his ordeal.

The train begins to pull away and whilst I was distracted by the squirrel sideshow, I didn't notice that an elderly lady had got on and was now sitting across the aisle from me, facing me and well within earshot.

"It's a great morning," I say to her with a smile.

She stares at me vacantly, and I assume she hasn't heard me over the rattle of the train.

"I said, it's a beautiful morning, isn't it?" A bit louder this time.

Still nothing. I laugh, and look back at the world outside.

48

I'm still eating the bacon sandwich I bought as I get into the office. I'm about an hour later than normal and the place is already full. I strut through the open plan office, but no one seems to pay me any attention, all wrapped up in their screens or huddled conversations. I don't let it bother me and when I get to my desk, I try to catch Ahmad's eye.

"Morning," I say as cheery as I can, without being too over the top.

He looks up, takes his ear phones out of his ears. "Morning."

"You, OK? Good night?"

He seems unsure of something.

"Yeah, I suppose. Nothing special. I wasn't expecting to see you today. After you left yesterday, Rachel got me into a meeting room and asked me to take on some of your work. She said you'd be off for a while."

I consider what he has said, but none of it makes sense.

"Don't know where she got that from," I say with a baffled tone. "No, you don't need to do my work for me, mate." I look at him for a few seconds and carry on. "In fact, if you've got a lot on, I'll take some of the load off of you, if you want?"

He looks at me like I've just told him I'm the second coming of Jesus. "Er, yeah, thanks, but I'm OK, cheers."

"We haven't really talked much, have we?" I say, trying to sound regretful but also aware I'm coming across a bit weird. "It's a shame, you know. We spend all day with each other and I barely know anything about you. Hey, you want to grab some lunch later maybe? Get to know each other more?"

He glances to the side and then back at his screen, uncomfortable with the eye contact. "Can't today. Maybe another time."

I laugh. "Come on, mate, I'm not flirting with you." I lean closer so I don't have to say the next part too loudly, "Your arse is safe around me. Besides, you're not my type." I wink.

That seems to break him down a bit, and he says with a sniff of a laugh, "It'll have to be tomorrow."

"It's a date. Well, not a date, but you know what I mean." I sit down and shut up, before I make him feel any weirder.

I pull my phone out of my chino pocket and check it. Still no reply from Becky, but somehow, I sense it's coming. Something is coming. Maybe I'll call her tonight when I'm home. For now, though, I need a coffee, so I head towards the kitchen at the back of the office. As I walk past Rachel's glass office, I can see she is talking to someone, but they are hidden behind the frosted glass door. I can't quite see who. She looks towards me and seems to do a double take. I wave back cheerily but she doesn't reciprocate. Instead, she waves to beckon me into her office.

This is unusual. I point at myself and mouth at her, 'Me?' She nods her head.

I open the door and step into her office, and immediately I see that the figure hidden behind the door is actually two people, and they both turn synchronously in their seats to look at me.

"Oliver," Rachel says flatly. "This is Detective Chief Inspector Carraway." My heart thuds. "He was asking about you."

49

"Good morning, Mr Pierce, I'm Detective Chief Inspector Carraway and this is Detective Inspector Kimball," he says, gesturing towards his colleague who remains seated and quiet.

Carraway extends his hand for me to shake.

"I wonder if you could spare us five minutes of your time, Mr Pierce?" he says with a reassuring look on his face. "Nothing to worry about, I'm sure."

Carraway is surprisingly young considering his rank, about my age I'd guess. He's wearing a dark suit that looks well-worn and dishevelled, and that doesn't hang well on his hunched frame. Underneath, a light blue shirt looks far too creased already for this time in the morning. His ruffled hair looks like he runs his hands through it too much. The dark rings around his eyes suggests a lack of sleep, no doubt in part due to his relentlessly stressful job. His pale face, a result of spending most of his time in the shadows of the city in the black of night. While everything about him screams the need for a good night's sleep, his eyes are clear and his hawk-like focus on me is unnerving.

"Why don't I leave you to it," Rachel says, standing and heading for the door. "I'll be in the meeting room to the left of here if you need me."

Carraway doesn't acknowledge her, but simply gestures for me to sit in the empty chair he has vacated, which I do. He begins a languid walk around the desk and slowly lowers himself into Rachel's leather chair, leans forward and places his elbows on the desk in front of him. His hunter's stare doesn't leave me for one split second, which makes me feel even more uncomfortable than I already did. I glance at his colleague sitting next to me. Kimball, was it?

Whatever her name is, she sits back in her chair, cross-legged, with slender hands holding onto each other and resting on her thigh. She wears a similar dark suit to Carraway, but hers looks much better on her. Her flat black slip-on shoes are functional, but not feminine at all. In fact, nothing about her look is feminine. I think perhaps that's the point. Regardless of the attempt, there is no hiding that she is very attractive.

"So," I start, trying to come off as friendly and conversational, in spite of Carraway's attempts to unsettle me. "How can I help?"

"As I said, Mr Pierce, we just have some cursory questions for you to help with our inquiries."

"And what inquiries are they?" I ask, genuinely baffled as to how I can help.

"Well," Kimball says, rifling through a small notebook she has taken out from her inside pocket. "Perhaps we could start by asking you about your day yesterday. Can you tell us about it, please?"

"I'm sorry," I say, trying to balance an affable smile with an equally affable look of confusion. "Am I being suspected of something here?"

"Just answer the question if you don't mind, Mr. Pierce," Carraway says in a deadpan tone.

"Of course, anything I can do to help."

I smile and direct my answer to Kimball, mainly because Carraway's stare is making me nervous, but also because she's so much more pleasant to look at. "Let me think. A pretty normal day to be honest. Came to work, as usual. Finished. Went home.

Stayed in. Watched TV. Went to bed. Simple as that." I roll my eyes as if in apology. "Not very rock and roll I'm afraid."

"Are you sure of that, Mr Pierce?"

"Yes, I am."

"And you definitely went straight home after leaving the office. You didn't stop off on the way home at all?" Kimball asks.

I think. "No, definitely not. I left work and went straight home."

"What time did you get home?" she continues.

"Erm, well it would have been around the normal time, I guess. Depending on the train I managed to get, any time between six and seven pm."

"Which is it?" Carraway demands. "Six or seven?"

I don't like his tone, but I have nothing to hide other than I had a few drinks, but they don't need to know that. I sigh and look above his right shoulder, as though I'm about to provide a more considered response.

"It would have been closer to six o'clock."

Carraway glances at Kimball, and I turn to her to see her response.

"Are you married, Mr Pierce?"

Officer Kimball! We've only just met.

"I'm married," I nod my head, frowning apologetically.

"And your wife would corroborate your story? That you were home by six o'clock last night?"

I breathe out a snorted laugh, confusion written across my face.

"Look, I'm sorry, but I really don't know what this is all about, and I'm starting to feel a bit uncomfortable here."

"I'm sorry you feel that way," Carraway this time, with not a hint that he feels any remorse at all. "But you see, we have a little problem here. Ms Bond, Rachel, she's your boss, correct?" He doesn't give me any time to answer. "Well, she said you left work around 10:30am, after she sent you home."

Did she?

Kimball carries on the line of inquiry seamlessly. "But you said you left at a 'normal time'."

"No," I correct her. "I didn't say that. I said I got home at a normal time, which I did."

I can hear my heart throbbing in my ears.

Carraway leans back in his chair and folds his arms. "Mr Pierce…"

"Please, call me Oliver."

"Mr Pierce," he repeats and pauses. An icy silence hangs in the room. "Can you tell me why Ms Bond sent you home early yesterday?"

"No."

"No, you can't, or no, you don't know?"

I'm getting annoyed now, and take a deep breath and sigh outwardly to try and express my frustration. "OK, look. I'm sorry, I'm not trying to be difficult, but it's a bit personal. My wife and I, we've…. Well, we've been having some issues and I may not have left them at home, if you know what I mean."

"No, I'm sorry, Mr Pierce, I don't know what you mean. Please elaborate."

"I mean, my issues at home, with my wife, they have been affecting me at work a bit. My performance, I guess. Rachel is a very caring boss, and she had spotted how…" I search for the right word, "…distracted I'd been lately. We talked about it and she told me to go home and try and work things out with my wife." Honesty is the best policy.

"And did you?" I sense I'm getting Kimball on my side.

"Did I what?"

"You went home and patched things up with your wife?"

I squirm in my seat. Why are these two making me feel guilty about something I haven't done? "Well, no. It's a bit embarrassing to say it out loud, but my wife went to stay at her parents' for a few days. With my son," I add. "She just needed a bit of space, I guess. But it's all going to be fine, we're already talking."

"So, if you agree that you left work at 10:30am, and didn't get home until your 'normal time' at 6pm, can I ask how you filled the time in between?" Carraway asks, the sentence heavy with insinuation.

"Well..." Think Ollie, think. "I'm not sure it wasn't later than 10:30, but anyway. I walked home instead of getting the train. I decided I wanted to clear my head, and thought a walk would help." The room is silent and Carraway and Kimball exchange knowing looks. "Actually, come to think of it, I did stop in a pub briefly, for a quick lunch... and a rest. The walk was longer than I had anticipated," I sniff a laugh at my own foolishness.

More silence, and I've watched enough police procedurals on TV to know that they are wanting me to fill it with something that will slip me up. So I don't.

"All right, Mr Pierce. I'm sorry for taking up your time," Carraway says, finally breaking the awkwardness that was hanging in the air. He stands and tucks his shirt back into his ill-fitting trousers, and extends his hand to shake mine. When we do shake, he grips my hand firmly for a lot longer than is comfortable. I internally kick myself for returning his handshake with such a limp response. The sudden stop in the conversation surprises me.

"No problem, anything I can do to help." I feel like I shouldn't say anything further, but the temptation is too much for me to bear. "Can I ask what this was to do with?"

"Murder," Carraway says flippantly, before turning to cast his baited stare at me. "The death of a young man."

I am visibly shaken. How can these people think I can be mixed up in something like that? I'm dumbfounded, and can't find the right thing to say.

"And you think I am involved?" I say eventually, incredulity rich in my response.

"Like I said, Mr Pierce," Carraway says, handing me his business card as he makes his way towards the door. "We just wanted to ask you a few things to help with our inquiries."

"Yes," Kimball adds. "And you've been very helpful. Thank you for your time." She doesn't try to shake my hand.

Carraway stops in the doorframe, turns, his eyes narrowing onto me. "There is one more thing, Oliver. Have you ever been to the Crown pub, in Hammersmith?"

I think for a second. There is something about the name that I recognise, but then it is a fairly popular name for a pub.

"No, I don't think I have." Their unremitting stares force me to fake disinterest and I look at an imaginary something going on in the office scene behind them. "Why?"

"No, I didn't think you had. Thank you once again, you've been very helpful," he says, finally walking through the door, Kimball following.

I sit back down in the chair heavily. My chest is tight, making it difficult to breathe. My head, dizzy with confusion.

50

The door to the office swings open, giving me a start and bringing me back to the present moment. Rachel glides in and perches on the edge of her desk next to me. I can smell her flowery scent, lush and sensual. I notice her smooth, toned calf muscles, contrasted by the electric blue high heels she is wearing. I realise I'm staring, and so I fight to look upwards to her eyes, bright brown, almost amber in colour. I smile, aiming for reassurance.

"Are you OK?" she asks, full of care, but she can't hide the intrigue in her voice.

I look at her and imagine her face as she orgasms.

"Yes, I'm fine thanks. That…" I pause, "…that was a bit weird!" A breathy snort escapes my nostrils.

"What did they want to talk to you about?"

"Honestly, Rachel, nothing. We've been having some issues with our neighbour recently. Nothing major, but she's now apparently made a complaint to the police, so they were just getting my side of the story."

She says nothing, and so I feel compelled to fill the silence.

"She's a batty old lady. Sad really. Got nothing else to do in her life. That's what I just said to them, and they agreed with me. What was it the detective said, 'we have to work with these sorts all the time'. What a waste of taxpayers' money." I shake my head for added effect.

She looks unsure, and wrinkles her nose as if a bad smell has just found her nostrils. "And they send senior CID officers to your place of work for a neighbour's complaint?"

I can see she's not buying it. I can't have her think they were investigating a murder, no matter how ludicrous my involvement is in it.

"She's claiming I threatened to kill her!" What the fuck Ollie? "I told you, she's nuts. I hope I never get like that. I should sue her. Defamation of character or something." Just shut up you idiot, you're making this worse.

"Is that why they were asking me about your whereabouts yesterday?" Miraculously, she sounds as if this is starting to make sense. I dig in.

"I suppose so." A thought flies into my mind. "What did you tell them?"

"The truth, Oliver, I told them the truth. That you were here when I arrived, that you were asleep at your desk and that I had to give you an official warning, and that I sent you home."

A vague recollection of that conversation pulls at my thoughts.

"Right," I say, trying to sound matter-of-fact. "Anyway, they said they'd go and talk to her and calm it all down. I'll probably go over to her later with my wife, take her some flowers or something. Be the bigger man, you know?"

She frowns. "Oliver, yesterday I warned you about your future here. You promised me you'd sort everything out and the very next day…"

"Rachel, this wasn't my fault, I…"

"The very next day," she says in staccato, her eyes closed in annoyance, stopping me in my tracks, "I've got police in my office asking about you. This really doesn't reassure me that you are sorting anything out!"

I need to sound disappointed, which is difficult to do because actually, I'm terrified. "I'm sorry, Rachel, you're right. But I promise this is all a big misunderstanding and just really bad timing as well." I shake my head sorrowfully, "I'm sorry to have let you down."

51

I leave Rachel's office, confident that I've smoothed things over with her. I pull the door closed and notice my trembling hand. I take a deep breath, trying to calm down before I head back to my desk. I notice the looks I'm getting from people on the floor as I walk by, so I try to look as confident as I can, minutely shaking my head as if to say, "Tut! What a laughable misunderstanding!"

I sit at my desk and stare intently at my monitor so as to not invite conversation from anyone. I notice my whole body is starting to shake and I feel like I'm losing control of it. I close my eyes and take another deep breath. I remember that I haven't checked my phone for a while, which has me lurching into the pocket of my chinos.

> Becky 10:13am
> Missed Call

I can't help but smile. My body relaxes. Everything will be all right.

52

I reread the message she sent me yesterday morning.

> Wednesday 6:12
> *I love you too x*

We can make this work, I know we can. I called her as soon as I saw her missed call, walking out of the office and heading into the corner of a quiet cafe nearby. Though it was a difficult conversation at first, with lots of silences and despairing sighs on her side, by the end of it, I had her laughing. Only once, but it felt good to hear. It bolstered my hope that everything will be fine in the end. I decided it best to continue to respect her need for space, so I haven't been in touch again, other than to text her to tell her I love her. She'd have seen it when she first woke up yesterday morning. I've tried not to think too much about Matt and whether she's seen him since she's been back. I've tried.

After everything at the start of the week, thankfully, it's been fairly uneventful at work since. I haven't seen Rachel, which can only be a good thing at the moment, and I haven't heard anything more from the police, which can only be a fantastic thing. I imagine it was all a case of mistaken identity. I decided that they had obviously picked up their real suspect on CCTV, but before that, the facial recognition system had mistakenly spat out my name. I promise myself that if I haven't heard an apology from them in the next few days, I'm going to give Carraway a call and demand one.

Or, actually, maybe I'll call Kimball.

In fact, it's Becky I want to call. We'd agreed to meet this Friday, and I can't wait to see her. She is going to leave William with her parents and get the train down tomorrow. She insisted we meet out somewhere, rather than the house. 'Like a date?' I had said with a smile. 'Sort of,' she had replied. Whilst it might only sort of be a date to her, it certainly feels like one to me. An important one. Meeting a woman in a bar and having a few drinks together. We'll chat and then maybe she'll come back home that night. Hopefully.

I press the telephone symbol next to her name and by the time I have the phone next to my ear, it's already ringing loudly. I imagine she is playing with William in her parents' living room, maybe a half-made children's jigsaw on the floor in front of them, her looking at the phone, smiling and leaving the room for some privacy. 'I'll be back in a bit, William,' she'll say.

"Hello. What's up?" she asks quickly, concern thick in her voice.

"Hi, you," I say, welling up with euphoria. "Nothing is up. I was just thinking about you and wanted to hear your voice."

"Right. Are you sure nothing's up?"

"Yes, of course, honestly, Becky. How's William?" I try to change the subject.

She sighs a loud, exasperated sigh, "Don't ask."

"Oh, well I just did. What has happened?"

"I don't know, maybe I'm overreacting, Ollie, but I worry about him." I suppose I should be worried too, but hearing her say my name makes my heart skip. She lowers her voice to a near-whisper, so as not to be overhead. "He's just, I don't know… different. I'll tell you about it tomorrow."

Tomorrow!

"I can't wait to see you, Becky. I've missed you."

"I've missed you too."

"Don't worry about him, he'll be fine. He's probably just reacting to all the changes, the move, new school, things with us, being back up there. I guess he's more perceptive than we give him credit for. But honestly, don't worry. I remember being a bit of a shit too at his age. Did I tell you I once shoplifted a Curly-Wurly when I was five?"

She doesn't reply, but I can picture her face.

"I can hear your smile," I say.

"Well, it's not exactly a major theft, is it?" she laughs.

"That's my point. Neither is a DVD."

"I know, I know, but it's not just that..." She's back to whispering, so I cut her off.

"We can talk about it tomorrow and we'll get it sorted with him. I promise. Everything will be fine."

"Yes, OK." Sigh.

"Anyway, I'll let you get back to it. I just wanted to hear your voice, and tell you I love you."

"I love you too."

"Sorry, I didn't hear that." I make the fuzzy noises of a crackling phone line. "Say that again."

She laughs. "Phones don't make that noise these days, you idiot! But I said I love you too."

I can still hear her smile.

"OK, see you tomorrow."

There is a long pause between us, but when she finally does speak, her tone has changed. Her laugh has faded and a serious, sympathetic tone replaces it.

"Ollie, you know it wasn't your fault, don't you? The crash I mean. It wasn't your fault."

I freeze, unsettled by the quick change of direction.

"Cal shouldn't have been driving and you tried to take the keys off him. You tried to stop it. The CCTV cameras showed that and the pub landlord said what happened."

Darkness closes in around me.

"Ollie?"

"I'm here."

I squeeze my eyes closed, fighting to stop the visions infecting my thoughts.

"Please stop blaming yourself."

I take a deep breath in and say on the exhale. "I'm trying." I can feel that despite whatever healing may have happened, the wounds in my heart have been ripped open again.

"OK."

"OK."

"OK. Well, I'll see you tomorrow then."

"You will." The thought cheers me a little.

"I love you."

That cheers me even more. Deadpan, I reply, "I know."

She laughs.

As I'm about to press the button to hang up, I hear her voice spring from the phone. "Wait, wait! Ollie, are you there?"

"Yes, what's up?"

"Where am I meeting you tomorrow? We haven't sorted it yet."

"Good point." I think for a little bit. "I'll text you a pin tomorrow, so you know exactly where to go, OK?"

"Sounds good. Bye."

"Bye."

53

Even though I've willed the time to pass, I feel I had a bit of a breakthrough at work today. It was one of the guys in the finance team's last day today, so there was the obligatory gathering for shop-bought cakes, drinks and excruciating small talk.

Except this time, it wasn't excruciating at all. This time, I felt like the centre of attention, as quite a few people took the opportunity to quiz me about the police visit earlier in the week. I basked in the role of the office rebel that was seemingly being bestowed upon me, and enjoyed the fact that one of the gathered, Harry I think his name was, said that he was glad I'd joined the company, because it had got exciting since I did.

Being a Friday, plans were made for a last-minute pub crawl and people seemed genuinely disappointed that I couldn't make it. But of course, I wouldn't miss my date tonight with Becky for anything. So yes, a breakthrough.

Even though I'd sent Becky the pin to the wine bar around the corner from work, I still wanted to come home to shower and change, rather than go straight there in the same work clothes. I have to put the effort in. No, tonight has to be special. I have to show Becky that it is special. It will be special.

She'd messaged me a little while back, telling me that she was on her train all right, and I liked the fact that she mentioned she had already bought a miniature bottle of white wine for the journey. Whether she was already relaxed about our date (for it is a date), or whether she was trying to relax because she was tense, I didn't care. I was confident that I could allay her fears and quite frankly, I was willing to agree to any demands she may have for me. I'd say and do just about anything to get her and William back. I need them in my life.

I had thought long and hard about where to meet her and while I appreciate it's a bit risky taking her to the bar where I met Yasmine, I figured it would be all right. For a start, it's unlikely Yasmine would go back there anyway, probably not wanting to bump into me considering how we ended things. Secondly, I like the bar. There is something about its allure that tugs at my insides. Something that makes me feel like a different person. It gives me the extra bit of confidence I will need if I'm to sweep Becky off her feet. Hell, I've already swept one person off their feet in there, so I can do it again. So yes, risky, but worth it.

When I think of my time with Yasmine, I don't really feel regretful or guilty for any of it. In spite of the callous way she finished our relationship, I still feel a certain fondness for her. We had fun and she helped open up something inside of me. In a strange way, she has helped bring Becky and me closer together. Well, she did for a bit, until other things got in the way. In retrospect, maybe I should have left it all to just that one night, but I won't castigate myself for not being able to hold back the temptation of another night, and another, and another.

I wonder where she is now. What she's doing.

I've given myself plenty of time to get myself ready. Again, I treated myself to the fancy soap in the shower, and gave myself an extra few sprays of the cologne that I know Becky likes. As for the rest of it, well it's a very simple decision as to what I'm going to wear tonight. I already decided days ago.

Before we left our old home, before everything, when William was still in nappies, we'd decided to treat ourselves to a weekend away. Her mum had excitedly agreed to look after

William for the few nights and we'd promised not to go too far, just in case we needed to get back quickly for whatever reason. So, while it wasn't the most romantic of destinations, our weekend together in Manchester was one of the best of my life.

I'd booked us into one of the most prestigious hotels in the city, upgrading the room a level or two beyond what I could really afford, and booked tables at the very best restaurants the city had to offer. We'd arrived into Manchester Piccadilly train station on the Friday evening and after a short cab ride to the hotel, one thing led to another and we never did leave the room that night. There's just something about hotel rooms. The next morning, with bedsheet-burnt knees and stiffened hips, we showered together in the large shower, making love again, before heading into the city for a walk.

After a long, relaxed breakfast in a French-style patisserie, we had wandered around the high-end shopping district, which is where Becky saw the shirt that I will wear tonight for her. It's definitely not something I would have picked out for myself, but obviously it had appealed to her for some reason, and after a short discussion on the pavement outside the store, I'd agreed to 'at least try it on'.

When I walked out of the changing room, self-conscious from the love-handle-accentuating tightness of the slim fit, especially in front of the highly fashionable and muscular assistant, Becky smiled her smile. The one that always did, and still does, makes my heart skip a beat. The one I saw across the room that very first time.

She'd made me wear it to dinner that night, and insisted it remained on, though unbuttoned, when we made love again later in our room. I still have such a vivid image ingrained in my mind from that night. The moonlight was pouring through the large window, soaking her face and body so exquisitely as she lay under me. I will be able to picture that moment for the rest of my life.

So yes, I had no difficulty in deciding what to wear tonight, which is why my heart sinks when, rifling through my wardrobe, I can't find it. I quickly flick through Becky's wardrobe, and while it isn't there either, I do stop a moment to take in the smell of her perfume that radiates from her clothes. I'm starting to feel like a giddy school boy on his first date. The butterflies flickering in my stomach.

Where the fuck is this shirt? Then I remember. I had also chosen to wear it the night Yasmine and I went to that club. Surely it can't still be in the laundry basket after all this time. I head downstairs to the small utility room where a pile of my dirty underwear and socks has been growing over the week since Becky left. Trying to block out the stale smell of bachelorhood, I step over them and lift the basket lid to look for the shirt. I pick up a pair of my trousers sitting on top and a waft of vomit hits me. What is that all about? I hold the waist of the trousers and let the legs fall in front of me. Chunks of white and orange cling to them, damp and disgusting. What the fuck? When did I throw up on these? Assuming it is mine. Did I wear these with Yasmine as well? Did someone throw up on me?

I chuck them in the sink behind me and turn on the hot tap, thinking it better to leave them to soak overnight. As I watch the hot water spray from them, a blurry recollection of a dark alleyway peeps into my mind. The vision seems so arbitrarily abstract, as though I'm recalling one of those realistic dreams that you have, but can't quite mentally grasp a hold of the next morning. But these chunks rinsing off the bottom of my trousers now, right now, in front of my eyes… they're real.

I turn back to the basket, and my heart pounds heavily as I see a white shirt next to the pile, crumpled and stained. I pick it up, expecting another waft of sickly smell, but it doesn't come. Instead, the unmistakable scent of blood. My vision darkens and I feel a light-headed dizziness overcome me. The shirt drops to the floor, and I can see the full extent of the staining. Speckles and splashes of red have dried on the shirt, as if someone has flicked a paintbrush across it. I might be able to convince myself that it actually is paint, if it wasn't for the iron tinge in the air and the unmistakable deep red colour of arterial blood covering most of the front of the shirt.

I stumble backwards and struggle to catch my breath. I feel like I'm going to be sick, so I turn back to the sink and heave the liquified contents of my stomach over the soaking trousers. My face sweating with the exertion, I look back at the shirt, willing it to have been a figment of my imagination. Willing for it to blink away. A familiar sensation of the sound of rushing water cascades through my head, and my eyes and ears cease to function.

I have no idea how long I've been standing here, but at some point, the black cloak fades from my sight, replaced by dots of bright lightning which I try to rub away but only make them flash brighter. I'm still drenched with a terrible sense of dread. A sense that, whatever this macabre discovery points towards, I must get rid of the clothes. The quicker I can get rid of them, the quicker I can stop the memories coming back and rooting in my mind.

I rush unsteadily into the kitchen and take one of the plastic shopping bags from a drawer, head back into the utility room and stuff the shirt and soaking trousers into it. I check the basket for more, and decide to put as many of my clothes in the bag as possible, just in case.

I look at my watch. I need to get going if I'm to get to Becky in time and I don't want to be late for her. Not tonight. I bound up the stairs, taking two at a time, and though I'm disappointed to be putting on a different shirt to the one I had planned, I'm overcome more by fear and confusion. I check my phone. No messages, so I grab my wallet and run back downstairs. I'm stopped in my tracks when I see the plastic bag in the middle of the utility room floor. It's still there. Not a bad dream. Just there, staring back in judgement. Questioning me. Are you really going to do this?

"Shut up!" I surprise myself by shouting at it.

My decision made, I run into the garage to where we keep the barbecue. It's been gathering dust since our move and so it takes me a brief moment to find the bottle of charcoal lighter fluid and the box of matches.

I need to take a short detour to the train station, but I know exactly where I have to go. Crossing the busy road, I keep checking the underneath of the bag, imagining tell-tale red dripping from it. Thankfully there isn't and the contents stay concealed from the world. Though I want to run as fast as I can and get this over with as soon as possible, I know I need to appear relaxed and controlled, in stark contradiction to the panic I'm feeling inside. As I walk by the parade of shops, I see a CCTV camera bolted high up on the side of the building. An image of Carraway's pale and insipid face jumps into my mind. I make an effort to keep my head down and my face unseen.

I reach the red brick pub moments later, and hold back a bit as a group of loud, laughing men walk towards the front door. When they disappear inside, I head around the back of the building. As I turn the corner, I check again for CCTV cameras and, much to my relief, there aren't any here, so I can carry on with what I wanted to do.

I untie the handles of the shopping bag in my hand and take out the lighter fluid and matches. I drench the contents of the bag with the fuel, and for good measure, I empty the rest of the bottle into the large industrial bin, already half filled with black bin bags of rubbish from the pub. I put my own plastic bag in the bin and bring a lit match to the exposed cuff of my blood-flecked shirt. The flame immediately whooshes, singeing the hair on my knuckles and hand. I keep watching, just to be sure that the fire takes hold and spreads properly. When I'm absolutely convinced the fire is burning strongly, I pull the rolled-back lid over the bin and stare as black smoke billows from the holes and gaps.

Satisfied of a job well done, I turn and walk away.

54

Even with the detour, I still get to the bar with plenty of time to spare before Becky arrives. The neighbourhood feels very different at this time of night. I suppose the office workers have had their after-work relaxers and have already headed home, to be replaced by a different sort of crowd. Flocks of girls wearing short skirts and cleavage on display, replacing the elegant women from the daytime. Loud groups of raucous men, wearing jeans, t-shirts and tattooed arms, substitute the suit-wearing professionals that usually strut these streets.

    I stop and take a moment to look at the bar before I walk in. I remember when it was a painful symbol of my role as the outsider, but now I feel I'm returning with the confidence of a conquering hero. I took on this city and I feel like I've won. I notice a self-assured strut in my step as I head to the door.

    Once in, I'm first struck by how busy it is. However, there is still plenty of space to snake my way towards the bar, which is where I head, as per usual. I check my watch. Still ten minutes until she'll arrive, and remembering she has already started on the wine and needing to calm myself down a bit, I order a bottle of the same micro-brewed beer I had the very first night I walked in here. It worked then, I guess.

    I take a large gulp and scan the room, taking in the many faces around me. I don't see Yasmine, which, while I wasn't expecting to, is still a huge relief. Like outside, the crowd is different somehow. Maybe she knows how this place morphs into something different on a weekend night, and stays away.

Anyway, I don't care that she's not here.

The air feels electric with the expectation of the unexpected. Of what the night may bring for the people here. I notice a pretty girl, a bit too short for me, chatting to a smarmy looking man. The body language suggests they have recently met, an air of slight awkwardness from him maybe. However, given the way she is staring unwaveringly into his eyes as he speaks, and how her red lips purse suggestively around her straw, I fully suspect these two strangers will be fucking each other in a few hours. Yes, the place is literally crackling with sexual intent.

They're welcome to it. I wonder if Becky and I will be fucking tonight? I smile to myself. I expect so.

Something catches my eye and makes me look towards the entrance. And there she is, looking absolutely stunning as I'd have expected. I see her tentatively step in and look around, searching the intimidating room for me. She scans past me at first, failing to find me, which gives me a few more stolen seconds to take her in whilst remaining anonymous to her. She is, by far, the most beautiful woman in here. I become unaware of the noise and bustle around me, and for a few sweet seconds, the world feels as if it is letting me have this moment all to myself.

Eventually, her gaze stops on me and in the exact second of seeing me, there is a wonderful moment where her face softens and warms and I can watch her mouth mould into that smile. I smile back and she raises a cautious hand in a quick wave before heading my way. I watch, transfixed and in complete awe, as she winds through the mass of people towards me.

I love this woman. Don't fuck it up, Ollie. Any worries I'd had about tonight melt away entirely as a wave of excited elation crashes over me.

Closer now, she's almost within touching distance of me when I feel a hand grip on to my bicep tightly, the force of which breaks the bewitching spell Becky has cast over me. I turn to see an alarmingly familiar face. He shouts into my ear to be sure he is heard over the din.

"Mr Pierce, you do not have to say anything. But it may harm your defence if you do not mention…"

I stare at him vacantly, the words going into my ears, but my brain not registering their meaning. What the fuck is going on? Carraway's dour presence seems so alien here. His mouth continues to move, but the noises in my head drown him out. My first instinct is to run. I stare at the enormous hand squeezing my arm, mainly trying to register if in fact there is a hand there at all. I look up at the square-jawed face of its owner towering above me, and any thought of escape quickly dissolves away.

"…Do you understand?" Carraway's shouts finally hit my eardrums. Is this really happening? "Do you understand?" he says again, more forcefully.

I look at Becky, who stands aghast, frozen in time. She is so close to me that if I lifted my arm, I could touch her beautiful cheek. "Yes," I croak.

Powerless, I can offer no resistance as a powerful hand pushes me forward and towards the door past Becky. I can't look at her. I can't bring myself to see her face. I stare intently at my feet, watching them shuffle meekly forward.

All I can hear is her frightened, heartbroken voice, teeming with panic, as she says my name.

55

My forehead hurts from the pressure of it leaning against the window in the backseat of this police car. I'd like to think that the chilling sensation of the glass will relieve and cool my feverish brain, overheating with a million different thoughts careering through it. But then maybe that's just one more thought I'm adding to the list, because it doesn't.

Ollie?

All I can hear is Becky reverberating through me.

Ollie? Ollie?

I've never heard such raw emotion in her voice. Confusion. Pain. Panic. One second, Becky and my whole life, happy and complete, stood in front of me. And then the next, it was all gone, ripped away by those few words uttered by Carraway. Yet, surely this mistake will be fixed. I'm sure it will. They'll have to make an official apology from the Police, which I'll insist goes in every newspaper and on every TV channel possible. I want Carraway, and all of these idiots, to be made to pay for the mistakes they've made.

I picture myself standing on the stairs of an imposing courthouse, Becky next to me, a group of faceless supporters holding banners emblazoned with various slogans like 'Justice for Ollie' and 'Who polices the Police?' I imagine a rolling ticker tape at the bottom of the twenty-four-hour news channels, 'Breaking News: Home Secretary resigns in wake of Oliver Pierce wrongful arrest', as a grey-faced, grey-suited man hurriedly exits through the shiny black door of Number 10, before it closes dismissively behind him.

You can't just go around arresting innocent members of the public. Especially for murder! For Christ's sake, there is a murderer walking around out there! There is a murderer stalking his next victim, anonymous under the shroud of the dark night sky. He's out there and I'm in the back of a fucking police car in his place.

I look out of the window and at the people walking through the bright lights of the city. Old and young. Rich and poor. Attractive and pig-fucking-ugly. But all with smiles on their faces. Eagerness in their eyes. The hands of their loved ones in theirs. Full of anticipation of their nights ahead. And I'm in the back of a police car.

Ollie?

I feel a hot anger rise in me. I lean forward as far as the seatbelt will allow me, poking my head between the driver's seat and passenger seat that Carraway is sitting in.

"You're making a huge mistake, Carraway, you know that?"

He remains silent, as does the driver, as does the beast of a man sharing the back seat with me.

"You're going to pay for this," I threaten. "When you realise the monumental fuck up you've just made, you'll be begging for my forgiveness. But I won't give it to you. I'm going to make sure you lose your job for this."

He remains defiantly mute, which irritates me more.

"In front of my fucking wife!" I scream, at which point the thug beside me puts a restraining hand on my chest and forces me back into my seat.

Carraway continues to look ahead, and then says calmly, "I would advise you to keep quiet for now, Mr Pierce."

Bile rises in my throat. "You're a fucking moron, Carraway.

A fucking idiot!"

"Mr Pierce!" he barks and turns to me with a penetrative glare. "Don't make this any worse for yourself than it already is. Just sit there and shut up. You'll have your chance to say whatever you want later."

And I fucking well will, you prick. I turn back to what is happening beyond my window.

56

When we arrive, the police station isn't what I was expecting. The movies will have you think that when the innocent man is walked through, he's shocked by the screaming pisshead scuffling with two or three uniforms as they push him to the drunk tank. He's disgusted by the haggard prostitute, her lank hair and petulant mouth ringed by angry spots, sitting resentfully and waiting to be processed. That there will be the incessant ringing of unanswered phones, drowned out by the ranting and raving of countless lowlifes across a vast building. But it's not like that. Not at all.

We walk from the silent car park at the back of the station, through a few double doors and down a series of empty corridors, until I'm stopped in front of a tall, long desk in the corner of a brightly lit room. Behind it another police officer stands quietly filling in a thick book in front of him. The silence in the room is disorientating and I don't know what to think.

"Hello there, Pete, you look like you're having a good night," the officer says cheerily.

"Could be better, Andy. How's the wife?" Carraway asks.

"Much better now, thank you. Now," he sighs and looks at me with a disapproving smile., "who do we have here?"

"I have a Mr Oliver Pierce for you."

The man identifies himself to me as Sergeant Andrew something, I don't really hear. He speaks for a bit, but I'm so totally bewildered, I absorb nothing.

"Mr Pierce, look at me."

I turn to Carraway. He sounds like he's speaking from behind a thick window, at the bottom of a long corridor, filled with water. "You have been arrested on suspicion of the murder of Mr Grant Pope on the night of Thursday 23 June on Parish Road, Hammersmith. As such, we can detain you for up to twenty-four hours and if we don't charge you, we may apply for further time to be allowed for your detention, or we will release you. Do you understand?"

Through the muffle, I hear the word 'murder' and that's about it until the final question. Something makes me nod my head.

I'm told to empty my pockets, so I leave my house keys, wallet and mobile phone on the counter, which they take and stuff into a large, padded envelope. I'm shuffled through a door into an adjoining room, my hand is placed onto a machine where my fingerprints are taken and a cotton stick is scraped along the inside of my mouth. My body, weak and compliant, is manipulated, pushed, pulled and probed as they like. I offer no resistance.

The Sergeant's voice is disarmingly compassionate. "Mr Pierce, I think you could do with some time to get your thoughts together. Someone will come to get you soon and, in the meantime, we'll arrange for a solicitor to be provided for you if you wish."

I hear him, but I don't respond. I close my eyes and all I see in the darkness is William, alone, staring back at me, a single tear spilling slowly down his soft cheek.

"This way please, Mr Pierce."

We walk back into the main reception and he gestures his arm to another door to the side of the desk. He unlocks it with the swipe of his ID card and I walk through it submissively. Lamb to the slaughter. The next room is a windowless, featureless corridor, flanked only by four thick looking green metal doors on one side. The door at the end, I notice, is wide open.

I know what this place is, and all of a sudden, I feel like I'm going to be sick.

"Number four, please."

I step into the small cell, stark and empty aside from a metal bed attached to one of the walls, and a thin, blue, plastic-covered mattress on top of it. I turn and watch the door be slammed with a loud echoing bang. The clanking of the lock rattles briefly and then silence. A silence so loud it screams in my ears.

57

"For the purposes of the recording, Mr Pierce did complain in strong terms about the length of time kept in his cell prior to this interview. Our written records show to have been one hour and forty-four minutes. Mr Pierce has also complained about feeling tired and feeling unwell with a headache. Mr Pierce has been provided with two pain killers for his headache and was offered the chance to gain further rest in his cell, thereby postponing this interview for a few hours, however this offer was duly declined."

Kimball can go fuck herself.

Carraway leans forward to rest his elbows on the table in front of him, empty bar a large manila envelope and a grey box I take as being the tape recorder.

Carraway speaks. "Mr Pierce, as previously stated in the custody suite, you have been arrested in connection with the murder of Mr Grant Pope on the night of Thursday 23 June, last week near to the Crown public house on Parish Road, Hammersmith. You have also been offered, and subsequently declined, free legal representation to be present. Do you understand?"

I can't believe this is happening.

"This is a disgrace," I growl.

"Please answer the question, Mr Pierce. Do you understand everything I have just said? Do you understand the reason you are here tonight talking to us?"

I look around the room. Grey walls on all sides, a small CCTV camera pointing at us from high up. No large mirror or one-way glass. Just the three of us, a table and the blinking red light of the tape recorder. The fluorescent light buzzes above us brightly and the room is noticeably warm. My back aches from lying down on the uncomfortable metal bed in the cell.

"Yes," I sigh. "But I'm telling you, you've made a huge mistake."

Kimball's turn. "Mr Pierce, can you tell us where you were on the night of Thursday 23 June?"

"I don't know," I say, throwing my hands into the air, overdoing the theatre a little bit. "Probably at home, where I always am."

"'Probably at home.' Where else could you probably have been?" asks Kimball.

"I don't know, but I was at home, and like I told you last time, my wife wasn't there, so I have no one to vouch for me, so of course, you're just going to keep picking at that aren't you, so you can stitch me up?"

"Mr Pierce, we are simply trying to understand your recollection of events," says Carraway, leaning back in his chair and crossing his arms. "Help us to understand. Please."

I feel my chest tighten, and I'm struggling to catch my breath. I focus on breathing, and have to consciously decide when to breathe in and when to breathe out, as if my natural body functions can't look after themselves. I can't get my breathing right, and I feel as if I'm starting to drown. In 1, 2, 3, 4… and out 1, 2, 3, 4.

"Mr Pierce," Kimball starts again. "Have you visited the Crown public house?"

I cough. "No. I don't know. I may have done before. I can't remember all of the places I've ever been in. Can you?"

"Fair enough. Well, let me rephrase my question. Did you

visit the Crown pub on Parish Road, Hammersmith last week, or indeed, any pub last week?"

I think for a moment. I really don't fucking know.

"I don't know."

"It's a simple question, Mr Pierce. I'm only asking you to cast your mind back a few days."

Arsehole.

"I think maybe a bar in the city near my office, but no, I wasn't in Hammersmith last week."

A silence smothers the room and they both stare at me expectantly for more.

"I don't even know where Hammersmith is, really," I add.

"Mr Pierce, how would you describe your state of mind right now?" Kimball asks.

What the fuck does that mean?

"What the fu…. What does that mean? What do you mean?" I ask. My headache is building, pulsing painfully with each of my thumping heart beats.

"I mean, how do you feel right now?"

"Well, very pissed off obviously. Very fucking confused as to why I'm here. Angry that you've embarrassed me in front of my wife, and possibly ruined any chance of me fixing my marriage." I feel a fleck of spittle hit my bottom lip as I shout the last few words, my anger and resentment building.

"But you are clear of mind?" she carries on.

"What the fuck do you mean, clear of mind? This is ridiculous!"

My eyes are burning now, the fluorescent lighting seemingly needling right through my eyeballs and into my brain. I feel my body trembling, and I try to hide it by gripping on to the table leg to help control it.

"Last Thursday, at the request of your manager, Ms Rachel Bond, you were sent home from work for unprofessional behaviour. How did that make you feel?"

"Wait, hang on a minute! You want me to tell you I was angry with Rachel, cut up by what has been happening with Becky, and this has somehow made me go and murder someone I have never met in my life? Seems a bit fucking convenient for you and this fucked up amateurish investigation, doesn't it?"

"Were you?" Carraway leans in, unable to stop himself bearing his childish-looking teeth.

"Was I what, Carraway?" I say defiantly.

"Angry with Rachel?"

Angry? I seem to recall I was fucking furious. "No, not at all," I shrug. "Like I said to you before, she was very considerate of my home situation and offered for me to take the day off to fix it. Tell me, why would I be angry with her for that?"

"And what about the situation with your wife? 'Cut up' you just said?"

Is it just me, or did he overemphasis the word 'cut' just then?

I see Becky's face as I was paraded past her earlier. "Of course I was upset. My wife left me and took my son with her. How the fuck would you feel if your wife did that, hey?" I'm unable to control my voice getting louder as I speak.

"I suspect I'd feel a lot of everything," he says eventually, making me feel very uncomfortable with how considered and accurate his response is. "I'd probably be very angry with her. Very hurt in fact."

"Well," I say quietly, slumping back into my chair and crossing my arms defiantly. "There you go. That's how I felt."

"Do you have a drinking problem, Mr Pierce?" Kimball asks, breaking the silence that descended in the warm room.

I'm feeling dizzy, not with the headache nor with the breathlessness, both getting worse with each minute. No, I feel dizzy from this jumping from one line of questioning to another that they're doing. I'm struggling to keep thinking straight, while thinking about everything that has happened to me recently.

Have they been following me?

Why did I have blood on my clothes?

Did they see me burn then?

"No," I say definitively, "I don't have a drinking problem."

Kimball reaches forward and picks up the manila envelope that has been on the table between us, ominous by its presence. She opens it and pulls out a large piece of glossy paper.

Have they spoken to Yasmine?

Have they been going through my phone?

"For the purposes of the recording, I am showing Mr Pierce a still taken from the CCTV camera at the Crown pub in Hammersmith on the night of the 23 of June. Mr Pierce," she says pointing at the figure of a man standing in the open doorway of a pub. "Is this you?"

I take the picture from her and look at it. It's very clear, not grainy at all, obviously taken by a good quality camera.

I'm numb.

What the fuck was I doing in there? It's definitely me, and it sends my head into a muddled spin.

58

"Mr Pierce, is the man in this picture you?"

I shake my head in utter disbelief.

"Mr Pierce, could you please answer orally for the benefit of the tape recording?"

"Yes," I murmur feebly.

I have to close my eyes to try and block out the bright light that is now searing deep into the back of my skull. My head is throbbing and my heart thumping. I can't focus. My mind is racing. I press my thumbs into my temples as hard as I can, to try to alleviate the jolts of electricity crashing through my brain.

"This photo was taken last Thursday 23rd June at 17:35, and shows you entering the Crown pub alone. Mr Pierce, do you have any recollection whatsoever of this?" Kimball asks, and amongst all the noise booming through my head, I catch a new emotion in her voice. Sympathy.

"No, I don't." I can barely hear my own voice. She continues, passing a few sheets of type-written paper towards me that I don't pick up. "I am showing Mr Pierce a written statement from a Mr Andrew Gunn, the landlord of the Crown. In it, he says, Mr Pierce, that you arrived at the pub around 5:30pm and were already heavily inebriated. He said you ordered a drink, visited the men's room, and then took your drink to a table in the corner of the pub where you sat alone. Do you remember this?"

While Kimball talks, my eyes are closed and I am back in the pub, picking up exactly where the photo left off. I remember the place now. Vivid recollections smash into my consciousness.

I remember desperately needing to use the bathroom. I remember feeling the hot specks of urine splash back on my hands as I relieved myself at a urinal. I remember trying to wash my hands, but there was no soap. I remember the slow trickle of cold water from the push-button tap.

"Bits of it... I think."

I remember how heavy my legs felt when I sat at the table. I remember my back ached. I remember spilling beer on my hands as I tried to grab my pint glass. And then I remember. Like a lightning bolt. Jay and Vinnie. A spewing chain of thoughts crashes through my head instantly. Drinking. Shouting. Anger. Crying. Outside. A motorbike's growl. I hear Jay scream. 'Vinnie! What have you done!' Whispered voices echo endlessly.

It was Vinnie.

It was Vinnie.

Vinnie did it.

Tell them it was Vinnie.

It wasn't us.

It was Vinnie.

"I didn't hear that Mr Pierce, could you repeat yourself?"

I'm staring into nothing, unable to focus on the faces in front of me. Blackness framing my vision and closing in. Disoriented.

"It was Vinnie," I mutter.

"Vinnie?" Kimball says with confusion. "Who is Vinnie?"

"I don't know. Someone I know. Met. A few times. He killed him. He killed the man. He's crazy!" I shout, stand up and bang my hands on the table. "He's dangerous you've got to stop him! You've got to get him in here before he kills someone else!"

"Mr Pierce, please sit down," Carraway demands.

"Stop him!" I plead, my voice breaking. I sit. "Stop him, please!"

"Mr Pierce, are you saying someone known to you as Vinnie is the murderer?" Kimball asks.

"Yes! It was him. He and Jay turned up." More images flash through my head. "They'd followed me there. To the pub. We left, and yes! That's right, I remember! He drove at us on his motorbike, tried to take my phone, I think. He crashed. I remember it all now! He crashed!" I'm babbling, a torrent of words just gushing from my mouth. "It reminded me of… well it reminded me of something else. He must have fallen off, and that's when Vinnie got him."

My vision tunnels again as the scene plays over me, the darkness toying with the edges of my sight. "He went crazy. There was a knife. Vinnie must have had it on him and he just went mental. We tried to stop him, Jay and I. We shouted for him to stop, but he didn't listen. He'd lost it."

I can hear everything as vividly as if it was happening in front of me right now. The liquid punches as the blade is plunged into his still body again and again. The demented screams. The voices. The panic. An overwhelming fright smashes across me and I burst into tears, sobbing uncontrollably, as the horrific recollections cement in my mind.

"Let's leave it there, shall we?" says Kimball, standing.

"No," barks Carraway. "No, sit down."

I don't know what is happening. My eyes stream with tears. My throat is so constricted that breathing gets even harder. I'm suffocating.

I hear a door click open behind me. I'm aware of someone else in the room, and when I look up, tears stinging my eyes, I see a plastic glass filled with water in front of me and a box of tissues. In front of Carraway, a laptop has appeared.

"Mr Pierce, please take a look at these CCTV images

captured on Parish Road that we obtained earlier today," he says soberly, and turns the laptop for me to see. I wipe my eyes with the back of my shirt sleeve, and I can see a silent, grainy, black and white image of the empty street. The camera angle is from high above from the other side of the road, and the scene is clearly lit by the street lights. In the bottom right of the screen, I see a digital timer that shows the time that the video was taken.

Apart from the timer, the image stays static, a photograph rather than a video. Finally, there is a movement as the door of the pub opens and a man stumbles out, just about correcting himself from falling flat on his face. Although I can't clearly make out that it's my face in the grainy image, I can see the clothes are the ones I was wearing. The ones I was wearing in the photo I was shown earlier. The ones I burnt earlier today. I stare, completely stunned at seeing myself on the screen gesticulating wildly. I seem to be shouting at someone. Through the tears welling in my eyes, I watch as I pull something from my pocket, and I know it's my phone. A few seconds later, a dark blur speeds across the video, which startles me and makes me jump back in my seat.

At this point, the camera changes, flicking perspective to a point further down the street. At the top of the screen, a pair of shoes, and at the bottom, the dark shape of a person, lying still on the floor. Next to him, the motorbike is on its side, half cut off from view, its front wheel just visible and still spinning wildly.

I watch in horror, unable to move, as the shoes run towards the man and kick him repeatedly. He kneels next to the rider, and picks something up from the floor beside him. Cold terror consumes my whole body as I watch the man on the screen lift the white object above his head before smashing it hard, again and again, into the prone rider. My heart breaks watching the man fight for his life, trying in vain to block each violent and vicious blow that rains down on him. A frenzied and sickening attack unfolds on the screen and I can't bear to watch it. I look down at my shaking hands that have gripped each other tightly in my lap. I focus on my bone white knuckles, locked tight together.

An eternity of silence passes. I lift my head, forcing myself to watch the horror. Mercifully, the attack has stopped. The rider's body lies motionless and the killer continues to kneel beside him, his shoulders rising and dropping quickly as he pants from his frenzied exertions. The man looks up directly at the camera, as if he knows it's there, and stares right at me, breathing heavily. Carraway pauses the video, freezing the terrifying scene.

I turn in my seat and lurch towards the waste paper bin in the corner of the room, but I don't make it and I vomit noisily across the floor.

That man is me.

59

I'm not clear on the chain of events that led to me being back on the blue plastic mattress in my cell. My body feels limp and weak, my brain devoid of any coherent thoughts whatsoever. I have no idea how long I've been here. My body is shivering, but I don't feel cold. I run a palm across my brow to wipe the damp, sickly feeling from my forehead, and realise that my hand feels like a block of ice. The physical pain I'm in is in stark contrast to the numb emptiness I feel inside, and the only clue that I'm actually awake and not in the middle of some terrible nightmare. I can hear a muffled shouting from behind the thick metal door, but I can't make out what's being said.

A chorus of whispers in my head, each voice battling to be heard.

What is happening?
What have we done?
We need to get out.

I can taste a familiar bitter acridity in my throat. A stinging sensation that is undeniably the aftertaste of vomit in my mouth. I must have thrown up recently, but I can't say for sure whether I have or not.

The video. The black and white CCTV footage of the killing. I close my eyes and through the pain and fog, I replay the scene, unravelling it in my mind, until the point where I am looking back at myself, shoulders rising and falling with the exertion. How can that be me? It's impossible. There has to be some other explanation.

It wasn't us.

We didn't do it.

I immediately think of Vinnie. I never trusted him. Not one bit. He could have had the video doctored somehow to frame me. I feel a hot anger swell within me. I'll make him pay for this. When I get out of this shit, I'll find him and make him pay, I swear to it.

The whispers continue to claw at me.

We did it. It was us.

We murdered him.

"Shut up!" I scream, tears erupting from my eyes and racing down my cheek. I wipe them away with the back of my hand. I'm shaking uncontrollably.

Who was the rider anyway? Why the hell was he out so late doing what he was doing? He was looking for trouble and he found it.

He deserved it.

He was trying to rob me, that much is clear. A thief and a bully, the scum of society. He is everything that is wrong with this country. Scumbags like him need to be taught a lesson. The rage grows inside of me.

He was worthless.

A waste.

What have we done?

If he'd been out mugging people all night, surely the police will have caught that on CCTV too? "He was rat shit! Worthless scum!" I growl, spittle flecking onto my chin. They will see that actually, if that really is me in the video, then I'm a hero. I've done them a favour. He was the one carrying the knife, wasn't he?

It was self-defence.

We did it.
We did it.
We did it.

I take a deep, calming breath. "That's it!" I say to no one. "That's my way out."

Self-defence. A sudden rush of relief washes over me, quelling the indignant fires deep within. I lie back on the bed, putting my hands behind my head. On the ceiling above me is a stencilled message to the occupants of the cell.

'Drug Problem? Fast tracking for treatment available in this station.'

I don't belong here.

I close my eyes to shut out the harshness of everything around me, and immediately I see a close up of my own face staring right back at me. Large and imposing, floating in the watery darkness that surrounds it. Hundreds of voices whisper from its mouth.

It was us.

An orange light rhythmically flicks on and off, momentarily bathing the face in its glow before turning off and returning it back to darkness. The tick-tock noise that accompanies each flickering movement gets louder and louder and louder in my head. My view begins to zoom out, the face getting smaller and smaller, but the chorus of whispers getting louder.

Look what we did.
We did this.
How could we.
Look what we did.

It keeps zooming out. I see myself sitting in the passenger seat of Calum's wrecked car. The flashing lights of the approaching police cars illuminate the scene, while I sit deathly still, pretending to be unconscious.

Self-defence. Is that why I did that to Calum? Is that why I moved him? To defend myself? Whatever it was for, I was right to do it. Was I right? Calum was dead, so what was the point in me going to prison? He would have understood why I did it. I'm sure he'd have done the same.

I was on autopilot then. My body was moving, but I wasn't in control of it. Something else had control of my thoughts and decisions.

The voices are getting too loud. A cacophony of chaos. I scream out loud to try to stop them. I feel tears pooling in my eyes, and I lurch up to sit again and I watch the tears spill to the floor between my feet. I'm in a desperately serious situation here, I see that. I feel completely overwhelmed. Utterly helpless. They're not going to believe me.

They won't believe us.

They're not going to believe Vinnie stitched me up, or that it was either the rider or me who was going to die.

We don't believe us.

I try to suppress the rising panic I'm feeling, but I can't. I'm fucked. I see it now. I hear it. I'm totally, completely fucked. The more I think, the more helpless and lost I feel. I'm terrified.

I look up towards the small window high above me. I could just about reach it if I jumped up, but the bars across it would stop me crawling through it. But the bars are what I need. I stare at them and the seed of a thought continues to germinate. A thought of a true escape. The bars will stop me from being able to climb through the window, but that is not the escape I want. They can help me with the escape I want. The escape I need.

Do it.
End it.

End it now.

Finish us.

I look down at my shoes and begin to undo the laces.

"You're just like ya dad was, ya coward piece a' shit." I turn and see Vinnie sitting next to me on the bed. "Fuckin' kill yourself as well, why don't ya."

60

"Sir, I think we should get him to a hospital. It isn't safe keeping him in a cell. Not in that state," says Detective Inspector Claire Kimball.

DCI Peter Carraway casts a critical eye at the floor in front of him, chewing the inside of his lip, deep in thought.

"As Custody Officer, I have to say I agree with Claire," Sergeant Andrew Gerrard says. "This clearly comes under the Mental Health Act, Pete, and after what happened in Southwark nick last month, I'm not comfortable with him staying here. We haven't got the personnel to keep an eye on him continuously."

Carraway looks between them, making his decision. "OK, fine. We're not going to get anything more out of him tonight anyway. I'll leave it with you," he says nodding at Gerrard.

"I'll get the Force Medical Examiner on call right away," Gerrard says, before turning and walking away purposefully.

Carraway closes his eyes tightly and tries to poke away the twinges in his forehead. "We'll have to change the charge sheet to voluntary manslaughter, you realise that? He'll be put away for a maximum of ten years. He'll be out in half that time if they get his head straight. He should be put away for life, Claire. It's just not right; nuts or not, he killed someone and his mental capacity shouldn't diminish the penalty."

"I know, sir. But he'll be off the streets and won't be about to hurt anyone else. Anyway, let's hear what the FME says. The way I look at it is that we could have saved other people's lives tonight, maybe even his wife."

Carraway sighs, but can't help but feel disappointed at how the night has panned out for him. "Thanks, Claire. Why don't you get home and get some sleep? It's been a long night, and we're not going to get anything more done tonight."

"Are you sure, sir?"

"Yes, get home," he says with a faint, beaten smile. "Oh, and Claire, good work on this."

"Thank you, sir," DI Claire Kimball says with a nod.

Pete Carraway watches her walk away down the long corridor, before turning and walking the opposite way towards his office and the hidden bottle of scotch. As Kimball reaches the swinging double doors at the end, she's almost knocked off her feet by another detective bursting through.

"Sir!" the young man shouts to Carraway, running towards him. "Sir, I've been looking for you."

"Yes, what is it?" Carraway asks, not stopping in stride.

"Sir, the Yasmine Irving murder. We've got a match on the fingerprints in her flat. They just came up on the system."

61
Sixteen Years Later

Still dressed in their graduation gowns, mortarboards in one hand, each other's hand in the other, the young couple stroll quietly together down the busy Birdcage Walk. It's a beautifully warm summer's day and the comfortable silence between them is exactly what they were looking for, and the reason for leaving the hectic post-graduation party behind them.

Half way through their second years at university, they were introduced to each other by a mutual friend, and from that day forth, they were inseparable from one another. The conversation that first night was constant, and the connection they began to feel was obvious. They quickly became best friends, and then one night a few months later, lovers.

They soon began to make plans for a life together after university, deciding they'd both like to escape the city and be somewhere quieter and more rural. They'd both managed to get the need for the vibrancy of London life out of their systems and now yearned for a sedate life in a small cottage somewhere, with a dog to walk in the fields and forests around them. They talked of the names they'd give their children and of the types of parents they would be.

They had worries about money and careers, like every young couple does, but one thing that was never in doubt for either of them was each other. They both felt that as long as they were together, they were strong enough to tackle anything life could throw their way.

They wordlessly stroll into the green fields of St. James' Park, and remain silent in each other's company as they cross the Blue Bridge. They would come here from time to time, both of them enjoying the tranquillity the park affords, and also watching the resident pelicans preen themselves on the shores of the lake. From the bridge, looking east, the park's oak and willow trees frame the water beautifully, and over them in the distance, the roofs of Whitehall and the London Eye give the only hint of the city that surrounds them.

A squeeze of her hand prompts the young couple to get going again and continue their way over the bridge. They walk past a couple picnicking with their blonde-haired toddler, and find a spot on the grass nearby to sit down.

"I love you," he says.

A beaming smile transforms her face, as she rests the side of her head against his shoulder. "I love you too."

"So, that's it then. School's out."

"I know! Finally! I can't wait to start our life together. It feels like it's been ages coming."

"Well, it has in a way."

The young mother is spoon-feeding her child, as the father looks on proudly. The warm breeze carries the distant sound of the toddler's giggles to their ears, and neither need to say a thing, both knowing what the other is thinking. A time in the future with their own children.

A few minutes of delicious silence passes as that thought roots deeper into their souls.

"I don't think I've seen your mum as happy as she was today."

"I know," he says with a smile. "I was glad she was able to make it."

"I don't think she'd have missed it for the world."

They both watch peacefully as a flock of birds take flight from the grass.

"Her and Professor Barnes were getting on well. Did you notice?" she says, nudging him playfully. "Can you imagine if they got together! You'd have Barnesy as your dad!"

"Oh God, don't! I'll have to nip that in the bud! Anyway, he'd be your dad too eventually!"

Their laughter eventually subsides and their attention is directed towards a small group of teenagers on the other side of the clearing, who have just started to kick a football around between them.

"Do you think your dad was there?" she says finally, breaking the long silence.

"What? Why would you ask that?"

"I don't know, I just think if he knew you were graduating today, he'd be proud and would want to see you at least. Even from a distance."

"I doubt it. Why would he care now? He left Mum and me when I was a kid and hasn't even bothered to get in touch once in all that time. For all I know, he could be dead." He sits quietly for a moment, before adding, "As far as I'm concerned, he is."

Inwardly kicking herself for bringing his dad up, she realises the mood between them has become cold. She knows it's a delicate subject for him. Even more so for his mum, who, during the one conversation she had had with her about him had said, 'He just wasn't able to cope with the life he had, so he left us.' She quickly changed the subject, making it clear they would never return to it again.

"I'm sorry. I didn't mean to bring him up. I don't know what I was thinking," she leans towards him and gives him a tender kiss on his cheek.

"It's fine," he sighs, but it's clear to her that it's not.

He watches the young dad playfully chase his son around the picnic rug. It's such a beautiful and lovely scene to see, and it provokes the very faint memories he has of his own father to appear foggily into his thoughts. He struggles to remember the details of his dad's facial features, having left him and his mum so long ago when he was still so very young. For some reason, when he thinks of his dad, he recalls being pushed on a swing by him. But even though his own recollections are tarnished, he can't help but admire the heart-warming scene happening in front of him. He is filled with an enormous wave of pleasure at the thought that he will one day be doing the same with his own child. With a steely resolve, he again reiterates his promise to himself that he'll be a better father than his own was to him.

He can see the wide-eyed excitement in the toddler's face, and he smiles automatically in response. Suddenly, a football comes flying across from the side of his view and hits the child hard in his face with a thud. It whips his head back and sends his tiny, fragile body sprawling to the floor.

Time stands still, seemingly taking a few seconds for his brain to register what he's just seen. He feels a violent surge of savage anger grip him, a splintering deep inside. A burning rage he has felt only a few times before. A rage he cannot control. The edges of his vision blacken. He shakes his hand from hers, and in one fluid motion, stands and sprints towards the group of teenagers. Violence burns in his eyes. His fists are tightly balled, primed for vengeance.

"William!" she screams after him.